"What are you doing here?"

Samantha stared at Blaize seated at the desk. "I thought you were in London."

"You wasted precious little time in getting here, once you thought I was gone, didn't you?" Blaize said with a nasty smile.

"What the devil are you talking about?" Samantha asked, her voice rising.

"Shh. Not so loud," he said, shaking his head at her. "My mother is only two doors away, and I certainly don't plan to let you disturb her further."

"I haven't disturbed her at all!" Samantha answered. What on earth was going on?

"I think it's high time you were honest with me," Blaize ordered, his eyes as cold as ice. "I'd like to admire your cleverness. I must admit, you had me fooled completely."

Samantha sat, her head spinning. Where had the soft-voiced Blaize Leighton gone— the man she loved?

Katherine Arthur is full of life. She describes
herself as a writer, research associate (she works with
her husband, a research professor in experimental
psychology), farmer, housewife, proud mother of five
and a grandmother to boot. The family is definitely
full of overachievers. But what she finds most
interesting is the diversity of occupations the children
have chosen—sports medicine, computers, finance
and neuroscience (pioneering brain tissue
transplants), to name a few. Why, the possibilities for
story ideas are practically limitless.

Books by Katherine Arthur

HARLEQUIN ROMANCE
2755—CINDERELLA WIFE
2821—ROAD TO LOVE
2905—FORECAST OF LOVE

Don't miss any of our special offers. Write to us at the
following address for information on our newest releases.

Harlequin Reader Service
901 Fuhrmann Blvd., P.O. Box 1397, Buffalo, NY 14240
Canadian address: P.O. Box 603,
Fort Erie, Ont. L2A 5X3

Send Me No Flowers

Katherine Arthur

Harlequin Books

TORONTO • NEW YORK • LONDON
AMSTERDAM • PARIS • SYDNEY • HAMBURG
STOCKHOLM • ATHENS • TOKYO • MILAN

Original hardcover edition published in 1988
by Mills & Boon Limited

ISBN 0-373-02948-9

Harlequin Romance first edition December 1988

SEND ME NO FLOWERS

Send me no flowers,
Whose blooms quickly die.
Write me no love notes,
And tell me no lies.

—Barbara Eriksen

CHAPTER ONE

'SLIM, darn you, come back here!'

Samantha made an abortive grab at the wet dog who had lurched from her grasp at the sound of the doorbell, leaving a trail of muddy footprints on her newly polished kitchen tiles as he dashed towards the front door, barking frantically. She grabbed a towel and pursued him, thinking dire thoughts about the plumbers for leaving that gaping, soggy trench in her backyard, and cursing under her breath the luck that had made someone choose this particular moment to come to her door out of all the possible doors in Los Angeles. It was probably just some blasted salesman, she thought angrily. Another two minutes and she'd at least have had Slim's feet clean. She caught up with Slim, flung the towel around him, and picked him up, clutching him against her sodden sweatshirt.

'Hold still!' she commanded, reaching for the door and pulling it open. 'Yes?' she said, frowning at the tall, slender man in the impeccable grey suit who stood before her, holding a long, white box.

'Samantha Bennet?'

'Yes,' Samantha replied impatiently. The man didn't need to look so surprised, as if he'd expected to see a regular woman and had happened on a circus sideshow instead. She knew she looked a mess, but she hadn't invited him to come to her door.

'I wonder if I might come in. There's something I'd like to ask you, and I brought these...' The box started in Samantha's direction.

'No, thank you!'

Samantha closed her door with a resounding bang before the man could get the box into the opening, flipped the lock across, and marched angrily back towards her kitchen, still clutching the squirming dog. Salesmen and their little tricks! She'd seen that move with the box coming a mile off. They were just like mice. They could get their whole body through any crevice they could get their nose into. It must take a hide like a rhinoceros to keep doing that, day after day. That one must work overtime; he was wearing a very expensive suit.

The doorbell rang again.

'Oh, no, you don't,' Samantha said grimly, as Slim barked and flailed his feet wildly. 'You'll stay in the kitchen while I get rid of that pest.' She shoved him through the kitchen door and closed it firmly, then hurried back to her front door, pushing the straggling blonde wisps back from her perspiring forehead. She jerked open the door.

'I'm sorry, but I'm not in the market for...'

Miss Bennet, I'm not a salesman,' the man said, smiling down at her in a friendly manner, the box now tucked under his arm. He held out a card toward her. 'My name is Blaize Leighton. I saw you on the television show last night. I only wanted to talk to you.'

Samantha took the card and looked at it suspiciously. Why would someone who saw her with Mark Westland on Hal Findley's television talk show want to see her? 'Blaize Leighton, President, G. B.

Leighton & Son, Investments - New York and Los Angeles,' the card read. Obviously an important person. She looked at him again. There was something vaguely familiar about the man, the arrogant way he carried his head and that confident little smile as he watched her, but as far as she could remember she had never met any Blaize Leighton. Maybe it was that little cleft in his chin that reminded her of Mark Westland. He obviously thought he had as much of a way with the ladies as that famous actor had had in his youth, the way he was eyeing her. And with that mop of mahogany curls and those dark, bedroom eyes he probably made plenty of conquests. He must belong to that Mercedes at the kerb. He looked thirty-five-ish. Too young to be one of the famous personages that Mark Westland might mention in the memoirs that Samantha was going to help him write. But why...oh, yes, that must be it! He was the '& Son', here on behalf of his father. Hal Findley had mentioned they might expect some attempts by Mark Westland's old acquaintances to either bribe their way in or out of his book, depending on their desire for publicity. An investment banker with some peccadilloes in his past would probably want to be kept out.

'May I come in?' Blaize Leighton asked, his eyes running up and down from Samantha's flushed cheeks, to her long, bare legs and frayed sneakers. 'I'm sorry if I've caught you at a bad time,' he added, one side of his generous mouth quirking upwards.

'I don't think there'll be a good time,' Samantha said coldly, feeling a little shiver run down her spine at the warmly approving look in Blaize Leighton's ridiculously long-lashed eyes. Obviously, this Mr

Leighton took her for a fool if he thought she would fall for that come-on. 'I am not interested in discussing Mr Westland's book with you now, or ever. If you saw the show, you heard us say there won't be anything harmful in it. Goodbye, Mr Leighton.' She closed the door again, only a little more gently this time, ignoring the sound of Blaize Leighton's voice saying, 'Wait! That's not why I'm here!' and the persistent ringing of her doorbell which followed.

'Some people don't know when to quit. Who does he think he's kidding?' Samantha muttered to Slim, who was still complaining bitterly about being restricted to the kitchen. She wrestled the overweight beagle back into her sink and began scrubbing the clinging mud from his feet, still brooding over the appearance of one Blaize Leighton on her doorstep. How many more of those would there be? She had known it was risky, taking on the job of helping Mark Westland write his memoirs. His had been one of Hollywood's more colourful lives, his reputation for adventure and swashbuckling romance as torrid off the screen as on. Even at the age of seventy, his hair thinning and his famous moustache grey, there was still a certain arrogant grace about him, a charismatic magnetism to his flashing smile and bright blue eyes.

'The old guy must have really turned on the charm,' Bill Grimes had said when Samantha had returned from her interview with Mark Westland. 'I've never seen you look so pink-cheeked and flustered. What's he got that I haven't?'

'Not a thing. I mean, don't be silly,' Samantha had answered, frowning. 'You two are nothing alike. He's spent his life charming women. You're a political cartoonist. You make your living with brains and artistic talent, and make a valuable contribution to society. That's much more impressive.'

'I'd hand you my brains on a platter if I could make your big blue eyes light up like that,' Bill had replied.

'You're imagining things,' Samantha had said, but she knew it was at least partly true. There was something very appealing about Mark Westland that touched a tiny spark off inside her. Why had she never met a younger man who did that? Bill was her best friend, of either sex. She admired and respected him. She knew he loved her and would ask her to marry him in a minute if she gave him any encouragement. But she couldn't. She had always planned on going into marriage, as she did into other ventures in life, with both eyes open and both feet firmly planted on the ground. But, even though she and Bill could logically be considered very suitable mates, something held her back. Even in a sensible, well ordered world, there had to be a spark to weld two people together, and for her, Bill did not strike any spark.

'Before you give up your brains,' she had said then, to divert Bill from a topic that made her uncomfortable, 'tell me what you think. Should I take the job if he offers it to me? Which I doubt he will. He's already talked to a man who's done several ghost-writing jobs very successfully.'

'Lord, yes!' Bill had said. 'The new girl on the Hollywood gossip beat down at the newspaper told me the phones started ringing as soon as word hit the street that Mark Westland had contacted a publisher about doing his memoirs. It's got best-seller written all over it. Everyone wants to know who's going to be in it and what he's going to tell about them. You could make millions.'

At that, Samantha had made a sceptical face. 'Ghost-writers don't make millions. They collect a flat fee and then quietly fade away. Besides, I'm not sure it's my kind of job at all. What benefit is there to humanity from some movie star telling scandalous titbits about a lot of other rich and famous people? I don't want to be involved in a lot of sensational muckraking.'

Bill was not deterred. 'Make it an as-told-to, then. You'd get half the royalties. Come on, Sam. Even with all of your high-flown principles, you can't back off from that kind of money. Think of all the good you could do with it. You could rescue dozens more dogs from the animal shelter, or buy that bus with the wheelchair lift that the old people's home needs.'

'I suppose so,' Samantha had said doubtfully. 'But I'd still have to have Mr Westland's promise that he wouldn't really hurt anyone with his revelations.' She had shrugged. 'Anyway, why should I worry? He won't pick me. He only interviewed me because Agnes May is an old friend of his, and she recommended me after I did that story on her elderhostel project.'

'Want to bet?' Bill had said. 'I'll bet he knows you've won prizes for your free-lance work, and that you've got a knack for writing about people that's second to none.' He had grinned as Samantha's telephone started to ring. 'I'll bet that's him right now.'

'Nonsense,' Samantha had replied. 'I only got home half an hour ago. That's probably the plumber, saying he can't come today after all.'

But it *had* been Mark Westland. He had picked Samantha. Moreover, he had readily agreed to her request to have her name appear on the book, and assured her that he meant to make the book amusing, and not harmful in any way.

'However,' Mark had said, with his deep, melodious chuckle, 'I doubt that anyone will believe that, even if we tell them. Hal Findley wants you to appear on his talk show with me. He says he wants to meet my partner in crime.'

The show had been on the air the previous night, and already one potential victim, or his son, had appeared. Apparently, Samantha thought, as she finally managed to at least partially dry the wriggling, shaking Slim, there were going to be a lot of people who wouldn't believe that Mark would not damage their precious reputations, no matter what he or she said. Hal Findley had been definitely sceptical, and so, apparently, had Mr G. B. Leighton's son. Oh, well, as Mark Westland had pointed out, book sales would be a lot better if people expected something really scandalous. They had agreed to say no more on the topic and to answer individual enquiries with the stock reply that the only purpose of the book was to entertain with the stories about the rich and famous people Mark had known. If people were still worried, that was too bad. They couldn't tell each of the hundreds of people who might enquire exactly what would be said. By the time the book was finished, there would be no mystery or excitement about it left.

'There,' Samantha said, finally releasing Slim, who treated her to a disgusted look. 'You're beautiful and clean now. Don't look at me like that.' She dropped the wet towel on the floor, pushed it around with her foot to clean up Slim's tracks, and then went to the sliding glass door which opened on to the small patio and fenced backyard of her townhouse apartment.

With a quick move, she bent and scooped up the tiny dog who had bounded through as she opened it. 'OK, Poco, it's your turn,' she said to the moplike little animal. 'Thank goodness I didn't bring a dozen dogs home with me. You two are enough to drive me crazy sometimes.' Not that she hadn't been tempted. During the time that she was doing a story on the local humane society's need for funds for expansion, she had been haunted day and night by images of all those pleading eyes and hopeful, wagging tails. Slim and Poco had proved to be more than she could resist.

Samantha had scarcely lowered Poco into a tub of fresh water when her phone rang.

'Now what?' she grumbled, grabbing for her wall phone and tucking it into her shoulder. 'Hello?'

'Hi, Sam. Who was that guy at your door a little while ago? Some old boyfriend back in town?'

'Good heavens, no, Bill,' Samantha replied, trying to hide the irritation in her voice at this latest interruption. Sometimes she wished Bill didn't live directly across the street and work at home most of the time. It usually made her feel safer, but at the moment . . . 'It was just some salesman,' she added. There was no point in getting Bill worried about her being pestered by Mark Westland's possible targets. If she did, he'd probably come running every time someone knocked on her door.

'He drove a pretty fancy car,' Bill observed.

'Successful, I guess. Listen, I'm busy trying to wash dogs. Since that rain this morning, that trench the plumber dug is a muddy disaster. Can you call back later?'

'I just wondered if you'd like to take in a movie afterwards,' Bill replied. 'How about it? It's Saturday night.'

Samantha sighed. 'I don't think so. I've spent all day getting things cleaned up so I can devote my energies to the book. Mark and I are starting Monday, and I want to get my thoughts organised before then.' She bit her lip as she heard Bill sigh. He always looked so thoroughly depressed when she turned down and invitation. She could picture him now, the droop to his thin shoulders. Well, she was not going to give in to guilt feelings this time. It was time he started facing the fact that she was not going to be his, and took out some other women. 'Why don't you give some other lucky girl a break?' she suggested. 'How about the new Hollywood gossip girl? What's she like?'

'Monica Williams? She's just a kid,' Bill answered in scoffing tones. 'Cute, but she looks about twenty-one at the most.'

'So? Go play the fascinating older man.'

'Aw, c'mon, Sam. You know how I feel,' Bill protested.

Samantha wanted to say, and you know how *I* feel, but instead she merely said, 'Just a suggestion. I've really got to hang up now. I've got Poco all covered with lather.'

She did so, and had just got both hands thoroughly soapy when the telephone rang again.

'This is ridiculous!' she cried, snatching the receiver up again with a slippery hand. 'Hello?' she snapped irritably.

'Miss Bennet, this is Blaize Leighton again. Please don't hang up before I have a chance to correct your mistaken impression of me,' said a voice so deep and soft that Samantha felt another strange little shiver run through her.

The man ought to record commercials for a funeral director, she thought crossly, starting to pour cupfuls of water over Poco with her free hand.

'Mr Leighton, I am very busy,' she said, hoping that she sounded as annoyed as she felt, 'and I don't think my impression was in error. I can't think of any reason someone would come to see me after watching the Findley show, except to pry into what Mr Westland plans to reveal about either himself or someone he knows, can you?'

'I certainly can,' came the quick reply. 'I simply happened to see a young woman who was so beautiful and charming that I wanted to meet her and ask her to have dinner with me tomorrow. There wasn't time to find someone to introduce us, as I have to fly back to New York on Monday, so I found out where you lived and came to your door. I also brought some roses for you. I'm afraid they're going to wilt if you won't see me.'

'Mr Leighton,' Samantha said, grabbing a dry towel to shield herself as Poco suddenly shook vigorously, 'that is the most preposterous story I have ever heard, and as a reporter I have heard some fantastic stories. This is Los Angeles. There are at least ten thousand women here better-looking than I am. Besides that, you're a stockbroker, not some crazy Hollywood Romeo. I suggest you go and put your roses in some water, and chalk this one up to experience. Goodbye.' With that, she hung up the telephone, finished rinsing the protesting dog, and then began to dry her, still shaking her head over what Blaize Leighton had said. Imagine him thinking she would believe that line!

The dogs and her floor all finally clean simultaneously, Samantha went upstairs to her bath to add herself to the list of things that were clean and dry. She caught a glimpse of herself in a long mirror and burst out laughing. Strands of hair were sticking out every which way from her long blonde braid, and the smudges across her face made her look like a blue-eyed racoon with a moustache. No wonder Blaize Leighton had given her that story over the telephone. He couldn't possibly have said it to her face to face without laughing his head off, too!

Samantha showered and dried her hair, leaving it hanging silky and straight below her shoulders, then put on a long, hand-embroidered Mexican caftan that was her favourite for lounging around home in the evening. She smiled at her reflection now. She did look several hundred per cent better. Not quite good enough for someone of Blaize Leighton's ilk to have actually tracked her down after seeing her on television, but at least presentable. Too bad the man was so obviously a liar. He had been rather startlingly good-looking, now that she thought about it: so tall and slender, but well built, with nice, wide shoulders. He had a nice smile, too, and beautiful dark eyes, almost the colour of chocolate. Which reminded her... she was getting hungry.

'Come on, fellows, dinner time,' she said to the dogs, who followed her toward the stairs. Suddenly both dogs let out a yelp and bounded ahead of her, tearing downstairs and into the kitchen, where they barked a frantic chorus by the door. Samantha followed cautiously. 'Is there someone out there, or is it just a cat?' she asked softly, as Slim's bark subsided into a menacing growl. It was dark outside now, and with the lights on inside she could not see. She flipped off the switch and moved silently over to peer out through the glass door, but it was raining again, the darkness so thick that she could see nothing. She was just reaching for her patio light switch when there was a muffled crashing sound, followed by a loud curse.

'It's a man!' Samantha breathed, her heart doing a flip-flop and beginning to race. She grabbed the baseball bat she kept propped against the wall behind her curtains, for what she had always vaguely hoped would be a *coup de grâce* if someone broke in, then turned on the outside light. There, climbing out of the plumber's trench and covered with mud, still clutching a mangled box of flowers, was Blaize Leighton.

'What kind of a booby trap is that?' he roared, waving his arm toward the trench, as soon as Samantha opened her door. He got to his feet and started towards her, scowling through a splotch of mud across his cheek and forehead. He stopped at the doorstep and eyed Samantha, who was still staring at him and clutching her baseball bat. 'What did you plan to do with that?' he asked, indicating the bat. 'Finish me off?'

'That was the general idea,' she replied, trying to keep a straight face as the humour of the situation struck her. Obviously, Blaize Leighton was not amused. 'Come on in,' she said, 'and we'll get you cleaned up a bit. Then maybe you can tell me what in heaven's name you were doing out there, besides falling in the plumber's trench.'

'Trying to find a way to get through to you that I'm serious about wanting to see you,' he replied. 'I'd better not come in now, though. I'll make a mess of your house. Here.' He thrust the flower box toward Samantha. 'At least I'll finally get these damned roses delivered.'

Samantha looked at the muddy, bent box, and at last could contain herself no longer. She burst out laughing.

'I'm sorry,' she gasped, as Blaize Leighton glared at her. 'I'm afraid I'm having trouble believing this is really happening. Do come in. I've already cleaned up after my dogs several times today. Once more won't matter.'

'All right,' he said, smiling slightly as he stepped through the door. He put the box on the table and sat down in the chair which Samantha pulled out for him. 'Are the plumbers having a war in your backyard?' he asked, taking the towel she handed him and beginning to wipe the mud from his face.

'I'm beginning to think so,' she replied. 'They discovered an underground leak three days ago, but won't have the right fittings to fix it until Monday. Now, exactly why did you choose to come that way instead of by the front door? The gate is locked. You must have had to climb the fence.'

'I was afraid you wouldn't take me seriously if I chose the easy way,' Blaize replied, smiling that slanted smile again. His eyes drifted over Samantha's form and back to her eyes. 'You are exceptionally beautiful, you know. Or maybe you don't. Maybe that's why I'm having such trouble convincing you.'

Samantha felt her cheeks grow warm. What an incredibly smooth talker this man was! No wonder he was already president of Leighton & Son. 'It's not something I think about,' she replied brusquely, annoyed at her embarrassment. She gestured towards

Blaize's thick, brown curls. 'You have mud in your hair. Would you like to take a shower?'

Blaize shook his head. 'Thanks, but I'll just go home and clean up. I've got some company people coming to my beach house at Malibu, and I'm probably going to be late as it is. First, though, how about putting those roses in some water and then agreeing to have dinner with me tomorrow? I'd hate to think I've gone through all of this for naught.'

Suddenly feeling very tense, Samantha turned away to look for a vase. What should she do? There was obviously no denying that Blaize Leighton was serious about wanting to take her out. But why? Could it really be just because he'd seen her and liked what he saw? That still was very hard to believe. But what if that wasn't it? After all, he couldn't make her tell anything she didn't know, and so far she knew almost nothing about Mark Westland's book. It might be interesting to go out with Blaize Leighton, just to see what he really had in mind. He was certainly different. Several notches above any other man she'd ever met when it came to persistence. If he was after some information, he wanted it very badly.

Her forehead still puckered in a frown, Samantha looked back at Blaize Leighton. The dogs had already given him their stamp of approval, Poco on his lap and Slim with his head on his knee, submitting with half-closed eyes to having his ears rubbed. Anyone who liked dogs couldn't be all bad.

'All right, Mr Leighton, I'll have dinner with you tomorrow,' she said finally. 'But that's all, and it's only because I regret your accident. I'm still not sure I trust your motives.' When her uninvited guest smiled broadly, her response apparently making him very happy, she felt a pleasant rush of warmth which did nothing to calm her nerves as the phrase 'pink and flustered' popped into her head.

'You know,' he said, that smile having lighted some flickering sparks in his dark eyes, 'right now I'm not exactly sure what my motives are myself. But once we've had dinner, I'll know what to do next, because I, for one, am sure that *isn't* going to be all.' He stood up and carried the box of roses over to the counter where Samantha stood. 'Are you ever going to open these?' he asked, setting the box before her.

Samantha eyed him nervously. She opened the box and carefully folded back the paper. There, still looking quite fresh, in spite of everything, were two dozen long-stemmed roses, the deepest, most beautiful red she had ever seen, the scent filling her nostrils and making her almost dizzy. Never had she received such a lavish bouquet of her favourite flower.

'Oh, Mr Leighton,' she breathed, 'these are really lovely! Thank you. I'm...I'm sorry I made it so hard for you to deliver them.'

'All is forgiven if you'll call me Blaize,' said that soft voice, suddenly so close to her ear that she could feel its vibrations.

'Blaize,' she repeated, casting a quick glance up at him and smiling briefly.

'Very good,' he said, stepping back as if aware that he was making Samantha tense. 'All is forgiven, and I'll pick you up tomorrow evening at seven.'

'Fine,' Samantha agreed. At least, she hoped it was. The way she felt was not exactly fine. She seemed to be getting a lot of unusual vibrations, and they were not all from Blaize Leighton's deep voice. Why did he make her feel so uneasy? Was it because of that strange feeling she had that they had met before, or was it because she was so sure that his real purpose in taking her out had nothing to do with her appearance? She shrugged. What did it matter? She would have dinner with him tomorrow and that would be that.

CHAPTER TWO

'I AM not all pink and flustered again! And I told you he was just a salesman because I thought I'd gotten rid of him, and I didn't want you getting worried that he was someone sinister.'

Samantha glared alternately at the second huge bouquet of roses and at Bill Grimes, who had appeared at her door as soon as the florist's van had left. 'My face is all pink because it's hot today and I had to race around three blocks with those dogs. I can't let them out in the yard in the mud.' She frowned and looked around her living-room. 'Where on earth shall I put these?'

'Here,' said Bill, removing a pile of magazines from the end table next to Samantha's couch. 'You'd better clear off all of your tables if that guy's going to send you flowers every few minutes.'

'He's not. He was afraid the others mightn't last since they had such a hard time of it last night,' Samantha replied, placing the second bouquet of roses on the spot Bill had cleared. Blaize Leighton had also said that they were, 'In anticipation of a lovely evening,' but Bill didn't need to know about the card with them. There was no reason for him to suffer just because she'd had a weak moment and agreed to go out with Blaize Leighton.

'I didn't know you were so crazy about roses,' Bill said, watching Samantha take a deep breath of the

23

flowers before she straightened from setting them down.

'My grandmother had a wonderful rose garden,' Samantha replied. 'I only wish I had her way with flowers. Look, Bill, don't go reading something silly and romantic into this. Mr Leighton seems like a nice gentleman, but I only agreed to go out with him because I was sorry he had such a fall in that stupid trench. I have no intention of seeing him again after tonight. Besides, he said he's going back to New York tomorrow.'

'Hmmph,' Bill snorted. 'People like him go back and forth from New York to Los Angeles like you and I go back and forth to the corner grocery shop. Unless those flowers mean absolutely nothing, you'll be seeing him again.'

'Not if I don't want to. I'm still not sure what he's up to, but I do know that one word about Mark's book and that will be it. I don't believe that line Blaize handed me, anyway.'

'Blaize? Guaranteed to start a flame in your heart?' Bill sang a few lines from the old song about not wanting to set the world on fire, while Samantha first scowled and then stuck her fingers in her ears.

'It's a family name,' she said when he had stopped, grinning at her discomfort. 'I did some looking into G. B. Leighton & Son this morning. It's a solid old company, and Blaize is really George Blaize Leighton, Jr. His father's been dead a couple of years, and Blaize is president now. He's Harvard business school and old East Coast money, and all of that good stuff.'

'All of that research for someone you don't plan to see again?' Bill asked sceptically.

'Bill, for heaven's sake, use your head! Phoney business cards and red roses are easy enough to come by, and I didn't want to find myself alone in a car with some weirdo, so I checked him out with someone I know who I thought might know him.' Actually, she had hoped she might find out something that would give her an excuse not to go out with the man, but if Bill was going to be so obnoxious, she wasn't going to tell him that.

Bill chuckled. 'I wonder if poor Blaize Leighton knows what he's getting into, pursuing a former investigative reporter?'

'If it's such a drag, why don't you hang around and warn him?' Samantha asked coldly. 'He'll be here in less than an hour. Now, if you'll excuse me, I have to get myself presentable enough to go out with someone who drives a Mercedes and wears Italian suits.' Samantha looked pointedly at Bill's usual costume of cut-off jeans and a T-shirt with a slightly risqué slogan printed on it.

'I get the picture,' Bill said with a grimace, removing Poco from his lap and standing up. 'You know,' he said, pausing by the door, 'I'd wear Italian suits every day if I thought it would make a damn bit of difference.'

Samantha's heart sank. Her upcoming date had her so tense that she had unthinkingly hurt Bill again. 'Bill, wait!' she cried, and hurried towards him. 'Please, Bill, don't look like that. I didn't mean that I think any more of Blaize Leighton because of what he wears and drives. You know I'm not one for fancy clothes and expensive cars. I'm much more interested in the person that goes with them. In fact, it's a darned nuisance to have to get all dressed up just to eat dinner. I'd be much more comfortable with you.'

Bill smiled crookedly. 'Thanks for trying, Sam,' he said, 'but I think I'd trade comfortable for whatever Leighton's got. I think he's got even more of whatever it is than old Westland.' He started out the door and then turned back. 'Do me one favour, though. Don't kiss him goodnight on your doorstep. I can see it from my window, and I'll probably be watching.'

'Of course I won't,' Samantha promised. 'If he tries anything, you'll get to see me deck him, if I can still remember what I learned from those three karate lessons.'

'That almost makes me hope he does,' Bill said. 'Almost.'

Samantha sighed, watching Bill cross the street to his apartment. If only the shoe were on the other foot. She would be delighted to see him kissing someone goodnight. Well, Bill needn't worry about tonight. If Blaize Leighton thought he could buy the right to kiss Samantha Bennet with roses and a dinner, he would find out quite differently. Now, what on earth should she wear?

'I guess this blue silk will have to do,' she said a short time later, frowning at her reflection. For some reason its simple, tailored lines, which she had liked when she'd bought it, did not please her tonight, but she chalked that up to her generally nervous state. Even putting in her plain pearl stud ear-rings turned out to be a trial, one of them dropping from her fingers and bouncing off behind her dressing-table. 'I'll certainly be glad when this evening is over,' she muttered.

The doorbell rang at precisely seven o'clock, and Samantha accompanied Slim and Poco to the door, her attempt at maintaining a casual expression thwarted the moment she opened it. Blaize Leighton was standing before her in a tuxedo dinner-jacket and black tie, a corsage box in one hand and a huge white 'stretch' limousine at the kerb behind him.

'Good evening, Samantha,' Blaize said, smiling and lifting one eyebrow quizzically as she stared dumbly at him. 'May I come in?'

'Yes, of course,' she replied weakly, feeling as strange as if she had stepped through a looking glass into a different world. With the black of the dinner-jacket accenting his slender height, and his dark curls shining above the sculpted angles of his face, Blaize Leighton looked impossibly, unreally perfect.

Once inside, Blaize handed her the box. Beneath its transparent cover was a white orchid, tinged with deep blue. Samantha held it in front of her, trying to dredge up something to say from a mind gone completely blank.

'Is something wrong?' Blaize asked. 'It goes beautifully with your dress...and your eyes.'

'B-but...' Samantha roused herself and frowned up at him. 'You're dressed formally, and I'm not. I didn't realise you'd planned a formal evening.'

'Don't worry about it,' Blaize said quickly. 'You look lovely. That colour is perfect on you. Your hair looks like spun gold beside it.' He smiled as Samantha continued to frown. 'I should have warned you. I forget that California is much more casual than New York. But if it's going to bother you, I'll wait while you put on a long dress.'

A long dress. He seemed to think she had a wardrobe full of them. 'I only have the one I wore on the Findley show,' she said. 'I don't usually have time for such . . . nonsense.'

'I'd love to see you in that one in person,' Blaize said, smiling that slightly off-sided smile, 'but, as I said, I like the dress you have on. Whichever you prefer is fine with me, as long as you're comfortable.'

Comfortable! Samantha chewed her lip, trying to decide if there were anything that would make her comfortable with this man. Something about his very presence set her nerves on edge. But if she was going out in that limousine with him in that dinner-jacket, she would have to put on the dress she had bought expressly for the Findley show. Otherwise she would feel miserable instead of just uncomfortable.

'I'll change,' she said tightly. 'Please make yourself at home. I'm afraid all I have to drink is beer, and that's in the refrigerator.' She hurried up the stairs, listening to the sounds of Blaize Leighton opening and closing her refrigerator, and wondering why she hadn't had the good manners to at least get the beer for him. It was one thing to be casual and another to be a complete boor!

Her fingers feeling as agile as ten thumbs, Samantha put on the white dress with its swirling skirt and halter neckline that she had chosen to set off her lovely turquoise jewellery.

'I guess it's lucky I had to buy this dress,' she muttered to herself as she fastened the catch on the necklace and replaced her pearl ear-rings with droplets of silver and turquoise. She glanced quickly in her full-length mirror, tucked in a wisp that had escaped from her top-knot, and then hurried downstairs to rejoin Blaize Leighton, who was standing near her television, drinking a can of beer as calmly as if he always did so in a dinner-jacket. Before Samantha could apologise for her lack of hospitality, he gestured toward the large framed sketch on the wall.

'Who did that excellent picture of you and your dogs?' he asked.

'Bill Grimes, the political cartoonist,' Samantha replied. 'He lives across the street. When he was first getting started, he went from house to house doing sketches like that to make a little extra money. I expect he'd command quite a price for one now.'

Blaize nodded. 'He should. I've seen his work. I envy him his talent. Is he a good friend of yours now?' He looked questioningly at Samantha.

'Yes, a very good friend,' Samantha replied, surprised at the question.

'I thought as much. There's a lot of love in that picture,' Blaize said, smiling as Samantha stared at him, open-mouthed. 'It's nice to know the calibre of my competition. I always work better under pressure.'

'Competition?' Samantha's voice squeaked, and she cleared her throat. The nerve of the man, thinking he could barge into her life and immediately be considered the rival of someone she'd known for years! 'Just what competition do you think you're in?' she demanded, her already tense nerves giving her voice a harsh edge. 'If you're implying that you and Bill are vying for my affections, you can get that idea out of your head right now. You aren't even in the game. Bill's a wonderful person whom I respect more than any other man I've ever met.'

There was a moment of silence while Blaize seemed to be digesting Samantha's words, his eyes meeting hers without flinching. Then he treated her to a combination of his slanted smile, accompanied by a devilish twinkle, and said, 'That sounds encouraging. Shall we be off, now that you've gone from perfectly lovely to absolutely gorgeous?' He picked up the corsage box and opened it. 'How about wearing this in your hair? You don't want it to compete with that necklace.'

'All right,' Samantha agreed warily, taking the flower from him. She was not used to having her arguments so completely ignored. No, not ignored. Reinterpreted. It was as if what she had said and what Blaize had heard were two entirely different things, but she doubted that was the case. He was definitely quick, and very devious. The instincts that had told her he had more in mind than a pleasant dinner were probably right all along. She had better stay on her toes and not let his looks and charm lead her astray.

'Here, let me help.' Blaize took the flower from Samantha, who was having difficulty attaching it firmly to her swirling top-knot, his hands closing over hers as he did so. 'There. That should hold all right.' He cocked his head to one side and enquired, 'Now what's wrong? Did I stab you with the pin?'

'Oh, no! It's fine,' Samantha replied, trying to smile brightly. 'Thank you.' He might as well have stabbed her with the pin. She could still feel the sensation of his fingers on hers, and the aftershock that had raced through her body, along with the realisation that this was the first time he had touched her, and that it was more the fulfilment of an expectation than a surprise.

'You're welcome,' Blaize said, picking up Samantha's limp, hanging hand and tucking it beneath his elbow. 'Now, if you'll relax and stop looking at me as if you're afraid I'm going to turn into a frog or some kind of ghoul, I believe we're ready for a very lovely evening.'

'It may take a while for me to believe you aren't,' Samantha replied, trying to look straight ahead and appear calm as Blaize escorted her to the limousine, where the chauffeur waited in an impressive, braid-trimmed uniform. If Bill was watching now, he'd already be feeling terrible.

Once ensconced in the white leather seats, Samantha took a deep breath and tried to remind herself that she was still on the planet Earth, and not in some other world. She was simply having an evening out with a very wealthy gentleman, something that was not strange, in and of itself, but only unusual for her. It was also a good thing to be doing, in terms of the book she would soon be working on, for Mark Westland had doubtless taken many ladies out in similar circumstances, and it would help her get a feeling for the ambiance. Even Bill ought to be able to understand the practical benefits for her of the experience, if he could stop feeling sorry for himself long enough to do so. That was one of his problems. He was always playing on her conscience, instead of being positive. It was really quite nice, for a change, to be going out with someone who was so self-assured.

'Now?'

At the sound of Blaize Leighton's voice, Samantha started and looked up at him.

'I beg your pardon?' she said, as confused as if she'd just awakened at finding those dark eyes staring at her intently. 'I-I'm afraid I was lost in thought.'

'I know. I was watching your face. It appeared that you'd finally resolved something. Did you decide that you might be able to enjoy the evening, after all?'

'In a way,' Samantha replied, although she felt uneasy at the perceptiveness of Blaize's analysis. 'I was trying to put things in their proper perspective. As you are doubtless aware, I'm not used to this kind of elegance. In fact, the kind of free-lance reporting I usually do often puts me in contact with the other end of the spectrum, as far as wealth goes. I was just reminding myself that I needed to know more about the privileged classes in order to work on Mr Westland's book.'

'I'm glad you found some way to make the evening tolerable,' Blaize said drily.

'Oh, I didn't mean...' Samantha stopped, feeling herself blushing scarlet. 'I didn't mean to sound so sanctimonious,' she muttered. 'I don't know what's wrong with me.'

Blaize chuckled. 'I think I do. You're just not used to thinking of yourself as someone who deserves royal treatment. Why not pretend for the evening that your fairy godmother has waved her magic wand and turned your coffee-table into a limousine, Slim into a chauffeur, and concocted me out of thin air? That way, you can simply ignore all of the practical aspects of the situation and have a wonderful time.'

'I'll try,' Samantha promised, fervently hoping that she could do so. Blaize Leighton certainly deserved better treatment than she had given him so far. Even if he was only doing this to try and glean some information, his patience with her was really remarkable.

For the next few hours, Samantha successfully put all of her anxieties on hold, enjoying the marvellous dinner, at an exclusive restaurant in Laguna Beach, overlooking the Pacific, where floodlights played on the surf which pounded against a rocky shore beneath them. The champagne that they drank was superb, the delicate abalone steaks and beautifully arranged crisp vegetables fit for any royal palate. Blaize kept the conversation light and general, making even ordinary topics entertaining with his quick wit and easy humour. When they went on to a club in Beverly Hills that featured a dance band, Samantha found that dancing in Blaize Leighton's arms was an experience that surpassed what she would have demanded of any fairy godmother, leaving her feeling for a time as if she were floating on a cloud of bubbles from the champagne. Then, suddenly, the spell was broken and the real world returned with a jolt that stripped all the magic away.

They were sitting out a dance at a small table by the dance floor, when Blaize asked casually, 'How long have you known Mark Westland?'

'Only for a few days,' Samantha replied, instantly wary. 'We haven't even started on the book yet. Why?'

'Just curious. I thought perhaps you were a particular fan of his. It seems a little odd that he'd pick someone whose background was as an investigative reporter to do his story, instead of someone who's done that sort of thing before.'

He's leading up to something, Samantha thought before she shrugged and replied, 'I thought so, too. In fact, I was surprised that he chose me. But I do plan to do a lot of research into his past, independently from what he tells me. I believe Mark when he says he doesn't want to cause anyone any pain, or I wouldn't do the book. As an added precaution, I'm going to do my best to make sure all of the facts are straight. Beyond that, I'm not prepared to promise anything about what will or will not appear in the book.' She followed her statement with a meaningful lift of her eyebrows.

Blaize did not reply, but stared at her in thoughtful silence, one forefinger rubbing the cleft in his chin.

The lack of a quick response confirmed for Samantha that her point had struck home. Blaize Leighton had been about to say something about leaving the Leighton name out of Mark's book. Her eyes narrowed. The nerve of the man, thinking he could influence Samantha Bennet with a few hours of fun with the beautiful people! He must be trying to figure out how many more flowers he would have to send and dinners he might have to buy in order to get a more favourable response. Well, she might as well let him know right now that his efforts were not only wasted, but that they made her darned angry! She glared at him and spat out her next words with icy precision, her voice rising as she warmed to her topic.

'How charming to find out that my original intuition about why you wanted to take me out was right. You figured that if you brought me flowers and took me out for a lovely dinner I'd be willing to tell you if something about the Leightons is going to pop up in Mark Westland's book. It must create quite a problem for you to find out that I have no idea. No doubt you're wondering what it will take to pursuade me to leave out whatever it is when I do find out. Well, let me tell you something, Mr George Blaize Leighton, Jr, you have tried to subvert the wrong person. In fact, I respond quite negatively to attempts to bribe me. There is nothing you can do or say that will influence me in the slightest!'

'Samantha, for God's sake, keep your voice down,' Blaize said, looking around uncomfortably.

Samantha glanced up and saw that several people at nearby tables were watching them curiously. She smiled wryly.

'Of course. We wouldn't want to shatter any of the illusions, would we? Let's keep everything as insulated as possible from the real world, where people are hungry and homeless and will never see a place like this in their entire lives. Now, if you'll excuse me, I am going home in a common, ordinary taxi. I've had enough of this fancy fol-de-rol.'

With that, Samantha got up and walked swiftly towards the exit. She had not got far when Blaize was beside her.

'Samantha, please, for heaven's sake, simmer down and listen to me,' he said softly, trying to slow her pace with his hand on her shoulder. 'You fling a ton of accusations at me and then stalk off without even giving me a chance to reply. At least let me take you home so I can get my side of the story in.'

'Why should I?' Samantha demanded. 'I was right, wasn't I?' Before Blaize could answer, she stepped to the kerb and flagged a passing taxi.

'No, you were not!'

Blaize roared his answer with such force that Samantha, startled, turned to look at him. At that instant he grabbed her arm and signalled for the taxi to drive on, somehow managing simultaneously to motion for the limousine to approach them.

'You're going to hear my side whether you want to or not,' he said grimly, unceremoniously shoving her into the car ahead of him.

'My goodness, you do hate to see even a small investment go down the drain, don't you?' Samantha said sarcastically, moving as far across the seat as she could. 'No wonder your family has millions.'

'My family and the Leighton Foundation are famous for their charitable works,' Blaize replied, still at a low roar. 'That, however, is not the question at issue here. You seem to be labouring under the illusion that I couldn't possibly have wanted to take you out for any reason other than to influence what goes into that book of Mark Westland's. Well, while at the moment I am beginning to wonder why in hell I did, that is not the case. Yes, according to my mother, my father did know old Mark years ago. She seemed quite upset when she saw in the New York papers that Mark was going to write his memoirs, and so yes, I'm rather curious about what Mark might have to say, because I know perfectly well that my father was no angel. He's dead now, though, and my mother, who isn't well, is the only one who might be hurt. But if there's any influencing to be done, I'll go directly to Westland. I agree completely that your job isn't to screen the contents to pacify people, but only to tell Mark Westland's story as honestly and entertainingly as possible. I have no intention of trying to interfere with that. The only thing I want to change is your persistent idea that I wanted to take you out for the wrong reasons.'

Samantha raised her eyebrows sceptically. 'So far, you haven't convinced me. Exactly when did the revelation hit you that I am more fascinating than Mark Westland's book?' she asked. 'When you found out how lovely I look holding a wet beagle?'

Blaize chuckled, a smile spreading slowly from his eyes to his mouth.

'You were more fascinating all along. All I've said is that I'm curious about the book. Why shouldn't I be? However, if you must know, the moment I climbed out of that trench and saw you standing there with your baseball bat, fearlessly ready to defend your home and dogs from whatever maniac was out there in the dark, my interest in taking you out became completely detached from whatever slight interest I had in the book. With that light behind your golden hair, you looked like the most beautiful avenging angel I've ever seen. I'd have done anything in the world to persuade you to go out with me.'

Samantha tried to frown severely, but a strange little quivering in the pit of her stomach made it difficult. That smile of Blaize Leighton's was so seductive, and his flattering words sounded so sincere. But how on earth could she tell if he really meant them? And why should she care if he did? He had just admitted that he came to her house for what were, at least partly, as far as she was concerned, the wrong reasons. For all she knew, he was still pursuing them, just shifting his tactics to suit the situation.

'So you admit you rang my doorbell with the intention of finding out what I knew about the Leightons' place in Mark's book, and now I'm supposed to believe that you suddenly changed your mind because you were overwhelmed by my beauty,' she said, lifting her chin and looking coldly down her nose at Blaize. 'I don't believe you.'

'I didn't expect you to,' Blaize replied. 'You seem to have undervalued yourself rather badly. I expect it will take me quite a while to change your mind about that, as well as to teach you several other things that you need to learn.'

'What other things?' Samantha demanded hoarsely as Blaize kept smiling and moved closer. She felt a tightness in her throat and her pulse quickened at the rush of warmth his closeness brought. 'D-don't you try anything,' she stammered.

'Try anything?' Blaize raised his eyebrows quizzically and then cautiously reached out and touched her hand with one finger. When Samantha only frowned, he took her hand in both of his and examined it thoughtfully. 'Goodness, my dear, you've been working like a field hand,' he drawled in an imitation of Rhett Butler. 'You'll have to try a gentler shampoo on those dogs.'

'Stop that,' Samantha said, trying to pull her hand free, at the same time avoiding looking into Blaize's eyes, which were sparkling with merriment. He was so good at this kind of thing. She knew if she looked at him, she would smile, too. He didn't need that kind of encouragement.

'No,' Blaize replied. With one hand, he held firmly to hers, while with the other he grasped her chin and lifted it. 'Look at me,' he commanded.

When Samantha did not comply, he pulled her toward him, until all that she could see was his wide, sensual mouth and the square jut of his slightly clefted chin. His lips moved.

'Samantha, look at me,' he whispered, the hand that had held her chin sliding around behind her neck. 'It's time for your first lesson.'

'Wh-what lesson?' she stammered, her eyes finally moving to meet his in desperate retreat from gazing

at those soft lips, the sight of which had set her own
lips to tingling.

'A lesson,' he replied, taking the hand he still held
and placing it on his shoulder, then circling her with
his arm and pulling her still closer, 'in being kissed
as a beautiful woman should be kissed.' With that,
his mouth found hers.

Some remnant of sensible thought tried to tell
Samantha to freeze and fight him off, but it failed
miserably in the face of forces that sent a trembling
warmth through her so swiftly that she melted against
him in response to the pressure of his arms. His lips
were as soft and warm as summer, the emotions that
soared within her reintegrating feelings of joy and
springtime that she had not felt since she was a child.
She nestled close, her hand going behind his neck to
keep him there. Very slowly, as if he were trying to
let her find her own way, Blaize deepened the kiss, at
first only touching her lips with his tongue. When she
responded in kind, he traced the outline of her lower
lip, pausing when her tongue-tip met his. She moved
hers back and forth, feeling the firmness, which
seemed to have a special way of communicating with
her own tongue that was fascinating. Soon, there was
an interplay that left her breathless. She could feel
fires building in her breasts, which strained to press
closer. When Blaize's hand moved between them to
cup first one breast and then the other, she let out a
little moaning sigh. She wanted his hand on her bare
skin, not outside the clothing she wore. Wild visions
of being stretched against him, their bare bodies
glistening in an otherworldly light, filled her mind.
She knew that he was having similar thoughts, for she
could feel the tension in his muscles...

'Samantha?'

The warm mouth was withdrawn, the words a gentle breath against hers.

Samantha opened her eyes and found herself gazing into dark pools fringed with darker brown that seemed to still hold her enveloped in their depths. She raised her eyebrows in a questioning little frown. Why had he stopped?

'We're home,' Blaize said softly. 'I'm afraid the lesson's over. You get an A-plus.'

'Oh!'

Samantha pulled back, trying to reorientate herself. With a rush, her mind began to try to function again, but its efforts were not entirely successful. This man had taken advantage of her, and she tried to generate enough anger to tell him so, while all the time her eyes kept straying to his lips, her pounding heart telling her that she was not sorry at all. All that she could think of to say was a lame, 'You shouldn't have done that!'

'Come on, Samantha,' Blaize said softly, 'you wouldn't have missed it for the world, and neither would I. Not that I expect you to admit it.'

'Don't be so...so egotistical!' Samantha snapped, finally able to regain some control over her emotions. 'All you found out was that I didn't need any lessons, after all.'

At that, Blaize threw back his head and laughed heartily.

'You know damned well you've never been kissed like that before,' he said, 'and my ego has nothing to do with it.' He leaned very close to her again. 'Some day, Samantha,' he said softly, 'you'll admit to me that that was your first real kiss. Right now, though,

I'd better see you to your door before the neighbours think we're going to park here all night.'

'Oh, lord,' Samantha said, suddenly remembering Bill's plea. She looked quickly around. Thank goodness! Dark-tinted windows kept the back seat of the limousine well concealed from outside eyes.

'No one can tell we weren't just talking,' Blaize said, reading her anxious expression and movements well. He got out and helped Samantha from the car. 'I'll be back to see you as soon as I can,' he said, as he escorted her to her door. 'Try to keep next weekend open.'

Samantha put her key in the lock but did not turn it. At the sound, her dogs barked a frantic welcome, but she stood immobile, trying to think of a good way to tell Blaize Leighton that she was not going to be at his beck and call. Finally she decided that there was really no way except the simple and direct, given that she was standing on her front stoop at one in the morning and she was not sure what Blaize might do if she went into lengthy explanations. She looked up at him with what she hoped was a haughty and forbidding coldness.

'While I thank you for the dinner and a mostly pleasant evening, I'm not going out with you again, Mr Leighton,' she said. 'Kiss or no kiss. I suggest you stay in New York and give your lessons there.'

Blaize chuckled. 'That's exactly what I expected you to say. But I didn't put the roses in water and chalk it up to experience, and I don't plan to stay in New York, either. I'll call you tomorrow.' He bent and planted a swift kiss on Samantha's cheek, then turned and walked away, whistling softly.

Samantha opened her mouth to tell him not to bother, then closed it and slipped inside her door, submitting distractedly to the enthusiastic welcome from Slim and Poco. She might as well save her words. Blaize Leighton on a trail was like a bloodhound on a scent—deaf and dumb to any distractions. She only wished she knew which trail he was really on!

CHAPTER THREE

'I THOUGHT you said there wouldn't be any more flowers,' Bill said on Monday morning, arriving close on the heels of the florist's delivery.

Samantha shrugged and turned her back to hide her annoyance. She knew Bill was upset at Blaize Leighton's attentions to her, but there wasn't much she could do about the flowers, and Blaize Leighton was enough to worry about, without Bill compounding the problem. He was obviously still intent on his purpose, whatever it was, determined to drown her protests in a deluge of flowers. Not that it would do him any good, even though the tiny miniature rosebush, covered with bright pink blooms, was perfectly lovely.

'I think I said something on Saturday night about preferring live plants to cut flowers that fade,' she said, trying for a pleasant but casual tone. 'Besides, I got very angry with him when he brought up Mark's book. He's trying to pacify me.'

'And succeeding rather well,' Bill said drily. 'I saw your face when you read that card that you tucked in your pocket so fast.'

Exasperated, Samantha whirled back around to face Bill. 'You're reading things into my expression and the whole situation that are not there!' She counted to ten and tried to smile. 'I am not falling under the spell of Mr Leighton's rather overwhelming attentions. He has, as I told you yesterday, gone back to

New York. Now, why don't you do me a favour and go home and attack the congress instead of me? I have to get organised to start interviewing Mark Westland at one o'clock, and I have several things to do before then.'

'Are you going to tell Westland that Leighton's been trying to find out if he's going to be in the book?'

Samantha shook her head. 'It's not Blaize, it's his late father he seems to think might be included. And no, I'm not, at least, not right away, although I must admit I'm curious about what kind of mischief an investment banker got into. I have to establish a good rapport with Mark if we're going to work well together, and I don't think it would help any if I run tattling to him about someone the first day.'

'I can see your point,' Bill said. He started for the door and then stopped. 'By the way, I was wondering. Did that limousine have a bed in the back?'

'Did it . . . Bill Grimes, you take your nasty innuendoes and get out of here!' Samantha shouted, picking up a small pillow and throwing it at him as he departed, laughing.

When Bill was safely out of sight, Samantha took the card that had come with the rose-bush from her pocket. A quick glance earlier had told her that it was not something she wanted Bill to see. Now she read it over slowly. 'To lovely Samantha, whose lips are as soft as rose-petals, in remembrance of a kiss I shall never forget.' She felt her cheeks grow warm as she, too, remembered that kiss, not for the first time. It had haunted her sleep. Now it was returning by day, vividly real.

'Drat that man!' Samantha cried suddenly, crumpling the card and flinging it on to the floor. Blaize

Leighton probably did this kind of thing so often that he had the whole thing programmed out in detail, so that all he had to do was tell some secretary to send the rose sequence to Miss Bennet this week. Well, it wasn't going to work with her. She wasn't a mush-headed romantic. She still suspected his curiosity about what Mark Westland knew about his father was behind it all, rather than any overwhelming interest in her. What, she wondered, did he try to find out from all those other women he swamped with flowers and charm? Were they so gullible that they gave him valuable information about stocks, so that he could engage in insider trading and make more money? Did they slip him news of products? Reveal unsuspected oil funds?

'Woof!' said Poco, standing before her, expec-tantly wagging her plume of a tail, the now chewed and crumpled card on the floor in front of her.

With a sigh, Samantha bent and took the card and tossed it across the room for Poco to fetch again. Poco had the right idea. It was only a game, and not some-thing to get so excited and upset about. 'Thanks for reminding me,' she told the tiny dog, who came prancing proudly back again, her new toy held firmly in her teeth. 'I always knew you were smarter than I am. Now, remind me of all the things I'm supposed to take with me to Mr Westland's house today. Let's see . . . tape recorder, extra tapes, pencils and paper. What did I do with that list of questions I wanted to start out with? You didn't chew that up too, did you?'

By that evening, when Samantha sat down at her computer to begin to transcribe the information she had got from Mark Westland that day, she felt that Poco might as well have devoured her list of questions. She had only managed to get through the first four on a list of over twenty. It was almost impossible to keep Mark on track, every little incident reminding him of something new and, she readily admitted to herself, completely fascinating. So far they had only sketchily covered the period from his childhood to his escape as a stage-struck teenager from the drab, dustbowl era Kansas farm of his parents and got his first job, singing commercials for a radio station in New York; but even that was an adventure. She feared Mark had spoken the truth when he told Hal Findley that there was enough in his life to fill several volumes! Keeping it all organised was going to be the key.

She put the first tape on her playback machine and listened for several minutes to the early discussion she and Mark had had about the book in general. They had been sitting on the lattice-covered garden chairs behind his lovely home in the Hollywood hills. One of the dozen or so cats who followed him about like a latter-day Pied Piper had been sitting on his lap, and he'd stroked it gently, smiling as he spoke.

'You know, Samantha,' he'd said, 'I think writing this book may be the best idea I ever had. I've already heard from two old friends I'd lost touch with over the years.'

'That's wonderful,' she replied. 'I expect you'll hear from a lot more.'

'Some I might rather not hear from,' he said, a dry note to his voice. Then he sighed audibly, and said very softly, almost as if speaking only to himself, 'But one other, especially, that I do.'

Samantha stopped the tape and frowned thoughtfully. 'I wonder who that might be,' she said aloud. Mark had looked so wistful, almost sad, as he said it, his expression withdrawn, as if he were remembering something or someone long ago. She would have sworn his eyes were misty when he'd looked back at her, but it had been only a fleeting moment, and he had offered no further explanation. Quickly recovering, he had smiled at Samantha. 'Well, my dear, where would you like to begin?' he had asked.

'A little about your early life,' she'd suggested. 'Everyone wants to know about the kind of roots famous people have.'

Samantha had just become thoroughly engrossed in her work when the telephone on her desk rang.

'Wouldn't you know?' she muttered. Her hand reached out and then hung suspended over the receiver. Could it be Blaize Leighton? He had said he'd call. Well, if it was, he was going to get short shrift from her, rose-bush or no rose-bush. He needn't think he could worm his way into her affections by deluging her with flowers. His motives were still highly suspect. She picked up the receiver and anwered with a brusque 'Hello.'

'Hello, beautiful. How are you this evening?' said the soft, warm voice of Blaize Leighton.

'Very busy,' she replied, trying to ignore the quick rush of excitement that set her heart beating faster. 'I was just starting to transcribe my tapes from today, so I haven't time to talk. Thank you for the miniature rose-bush. It's very pretty. Goodbye, Mr Leighton.' She started to return the receiver to its cradle, but the unmistakable sound of Blaize's laughter drew it back to her ear like a magnet. 'What's so funny?' she demanded.

'You are. That is exactly what I guessed you'd say,' Blaize replied.

'If you already knew, why bother to call?' Samantha asked, wishing she sounded as annoyed as she should, but finding the sound of Blaize's laughter unsettlingly pleasant.

'So I could hear your voice,' Blaize said, still chuckling. 'Let's see if I'm right about something else. Did you tear the card into a million tiny bits and throw it into the waste-can?'

For a moment, Samantha was so surprised that she did not answer. Was Blaize some kind of clairvoyant, or was she really that predictable? He was certainly close enough on that one. Close, but not quite right.

'No,' she replied, 'I did not.'

'Hmmm. Well, I doubt you've tucked it under your pillow. Maybe you just tossed it out without shredding it. Is that it?'

'Do you really want to know?' Samantha asked. 'If I tell you, will you let me get back to work?'

'Sooner than if you don't,' Blaize replied. 'Come on, confess.'

'I wadded it up into a ball and threw it for Poco to fetch,' Samantha said, finding herself unable to repress a smile as Blaize once again laughed heartily. What a very strange man he was!

'That's wonderful,' he said a moment later. 'Better than my version. Now, I have a suggestion for you, if Poco hasn't chewed it to bits by now.'

'What's that?'

'Find it, flatten it out again and tuck it into a dictionary or something heavy. Some day you'll wish you'd kept it.'

'Oh, for heaven's sake!' Samantha exploded. 'You must think I'm some kind of a romantic adolescent. In case you didn't know, I'm twenty-seven years old, and long past the stage of tucking mementoes into books. I suppose if I'd shredded it, you'd tell me to glue it back together?'

'No, I'd tell you to put the pieces into a plastic bag and keep them,' Blaize replied, his voice still tinged with laughter. Then, suddenly, that voice became very soft again. 'I don't think you're an adolescent, but I do think you're a romantic in disguise. In fact, I know you are. But the reason I want you to keep the card is that some day, many years from now, it will be nice for us to have it to look at and remember this time when we first began to know each other.'

There was a long silence at Samantha's end, for she was sitting and staring into space, wondering what on earth she should say to a pronouncement like that, and at the same time as uneasy as if an astrologer had made some dire forecast. While she knew it couldn't possibly come true, it was still disturbing.

'Samantha?' came Blaize's voice again.

'I-I'm here,' she answered hesitantly.

'I'll let you get back to work now. Don't stay up too late. I'll talk to you tomorrow.'

'A-all right,' Samantha said.

'Goodnight, sweetheart.'

'Goodnight, Blaize.'

After Samantha had hung up her phone, she shook her head, trying to clear away what felt like a fog enveloping her mind. What kind of hypnotic effect did that voice of Blaize's have on her? He almost had her believing that they were going to have a future together! That was a ridiculous idea. Totally ridiculous! He was the wildest romantic she had ever met, rich, spoiled, and completely detached from the world of those whose fortunes left them with no choice but to work endless hours at some demeaning job, if they had any job at all. Not only that, but it was more than likely that all of his efforts were still aimed at keeping the name of Leighton out of Mark Westland's book. He certainly took her for a fool if he thought she believed his story of being suddenly overwhelmed by her beauty! Next time he called, she would tell him exactly that. She flipped on her transcribing machine and listened for a few minutes, then suddenly turned it off, jerked off her headpiece, and stood up, frowning. She was going to take the dogs for a walk until her head cleared again. There definitely was something supernatural going on here. For a few minutes, she had imagined that Mark Westland's voice sounded exactly like Blaize Leighton's!

The next morning, when the florist's van arrived, Samantha's only surprise was that Bill was not right on its heels. This time the miniature roses were yellow. 'To match the golden hair that I dream of every night,' said the card.

'What nonsense!' Samantha muttered, frowning as she discovered her hand unconsciously fingering a lock of hair. She eyed the card a moment, then walked into her kitchen and tore it into bits, watching with satisfaction as they showered into her waste-basket. Blaize probably thought that after last night she'd start believing his romantic nonsense and be more reluctant to destroy the card. Well, this ought to make her a little less predictable for him when he called, as he probably would. He was certainly predictable enough. When her telephone rang at precisely seven that evening she answered it brusquely.

'Hello, Blaize. I got the yellow rose-bush. Thank you. I tore up the card. Goodbye.' She held the receiver away from her ear, awaiting Blaize's laughter.

'Samantha! What in hell is going on?' cried a loud voice, unmistakably that of Bill Grimes.

'Bill?' With a shudder, Samantha returned the receiver to her ear, feeling her heart plummet into her shoes. 'I was expecting a call from...that pest of a Blaize Leighton,' she said hoarsely.

'Obviously,' came the dry reply. 'Maybe I'd better hang up so he doesn't get a busy signal.'

'Don't be silly,' Samantha said, recovering her aplomb. 'As you could tell from what I said, I wasn't waiting with baited breath. Where were you today?'

'I got a call from Monica early this morning. A certain ageing beauty queen got on her case last night for something she said in her column. She needed comforting, so I went over and took her out to brunch. Poor kid's a little naïve to deal with some of those sharks. How are you and Westland getting along?'

'We're getting along fine, but progress is slow. I think we've only got up to about his twentieth year, which leaves fifty to go. Did you know his first big break was as a song and dance man in a Broadway musical back in the thirties?'

'No kidding? I never knew he could dance. Have you asked him to demonstrate for you?'

Samantha laughed. 'I didn't have to, he did it spontaneously. And he's still pretty good. I just hope I'm that agile when I'm his age.'

'I wish I was now,' Bill replied. 'Well, I was just checking to see if everything's all right over there. I guess it is if you got another rose-bush. I'll let you go now and get ready for your lover boy to call.'

'He is *not* my lover boy! And I'm going to tell him tonight, if he calls, to quit sending things. See you tomorrow.'

Not, Samantha reflected as she hung up, that it was likely to do much good to tell Blaize anything. He would doubtless do exactly as he pleased, anyway. She set to work on her tapes, but found it difficult to concentrate, her eyes drifting frequently to the telephone on her desk. Why didn't Blaize call and get it over with?

But midnight came, and there had been no call. Samantha went to bed, feeling strangely uneasy. It was, she mused while lying in the dark, wide awake, very much like waiting for the other shoe to drop. Probably part of some plan of Blaize's to keep her on edge. But he had said he'd talk to her tomorrow. She might find him annoying and devious, but she hoped nothing had happened to him. Suddenly her bedside telephone rang and she lurched across the bed and grabbed it before it could ring twice.

'Hello?'

'Hello, sweetheart. Sorry to call so late, but I was held up at the most deadly boring dinner party I've ever been to. All I could think of was how much I'd rather be talking to you. Did I wake you?'

'N-no,' Samantha stammered. At the sound of Blaize's deep voice she had felt the most ridiculous rush of relief. It had left her almost breathless. 'I . . . I just finished my work for the day,' she added, sitting up and reaching to turn on her light.

'Are you in bed?' Blaize's voice was soft and seductive.

Samantha frowned at the telephone. She knew perfectly well what Blaize was trying to do. Insinuate himself into bed with her via long distance. Well, it wouldn't work.

'No,' she replied, 'I'm still dressed.'

Blaize chuckled. 'Samantha, don't lie to me. You *are* in bed, and I can picture you there, with that beautiful hair streaming out behind you on the pillow. See if you can picture me, lying beside you.'

'In your dinner-jacket or your muddy suit?' Samantha asked sarcastically, trying very hard not to picture Blaize Leighton at all.

'Try dark blue pyjama bottoms,' Blaize replied, undaunted. 'Let's see, I have a moderate amount of hair on my chest and a mole on my left shoulder. Does that help?'

'I'm spellbound,' Samantha replied, her best efforts at sounding coldly detached not entirely successful. The last thing she wanted was for Blaize to guess that his blasted trick was working. As he described himself, she could visualise him so clearly that it seemed she might actually reach out and touch him.

'Good,' Blaize said, as if he knew he was succeeding. 'Now, snuggle up and tell me what you did today. Did the plumber fill in his trench?'

Samantha sighed and laid back against her pillows. Why bother to argue? Blaize certainly couldn't see her, and it was rather nice, pretending...

'He did that yesterday,' she replied, 'but it's still a mess. I need to replant the grass now. Why don't you send me a box of grass seed instead of another rose-bush? Oh, I almost forgot, thank you for the yellow one. I tore up the card.' She waited for Blaize to laugh, but instead he sighed.

'Such a slow learner. I guess I'll have to bring you some duplicates. I'll be back on Saturday. What shall we do? Go to Disneyland?'

What had momentarily been a pleasant fantasy turned into sudden tension. Blaize was going to be back on Saturday? Even though she'd told him she would not go out with him again, he was coming back? Blaize Leighton on her doorstep was quite a different thing from Blaize Leighton three thousand miles away, talking to her on the telephone. He wanted to go to Disneyland? Didn't he ever think of anything serious?

'I told you on Sunday that I'm not going out with you again, and I certainly don't want to go to Disneyland. Why is it you never pay any attention to what I say?' Samantha demanded crossly.

'Because you don't mean what you say,' Blaize replied, his voice gentle. 'Come and put your head on my shoulder and tell me why you don't want to go to Disneyland.'

'Because...' Samantha began. She stopped. He was tricking her again. He'd gone right by the fact that she wasn't going out with him to her other statement, which she should have been smart enough to not have made in the first place. And now he had her thinking about putting her head on his bare shoulder, and she didn't want to think about that, either. How had he got her so confused?

'Why because?' the soft voice asked again.

'Oh, never mind!' Samantha cried. 'I'm not going anywhere with you. Goodbye!'

She replaced the receiver with a resounding thump and then buried her face in her pillow, her hands clenched and her eyes moist with unshed tears. What was wrong with her? Why was she so upset? It seemed that each time Blaize called, she ended up feeling this way.

In the morning, Samantha felt as if she had not slept a wink. She tried to concentrate on her work, but one ear was cocked for the ring of her doorbell announcing the arrival of the florist's daily delivery. No ring was heard. Bill did not even put in his usual appearance.

'Maybe Monica had another trauma,' she muttered to herself. If Bill was getting interested in another woman, that was fine with her. That would be one less problem for her to worry about. Maybe even Blaize Leighton had finally given up, in which case she had no problems left at all. Then why did she feel so awful? Maybe if she got busy she would feel better. She would stop at the library on her way to see Mark Westland, and see if there were some stories about him in the old movie magazines that used to be so popular.

'You look a bit peaky today, Samantha,' Mark Westland commented as soon as they were once again seated in comfortable lounge chairs on his patio, a pot of coffee on the low table between them. 'Don't you feel well? If not, we can take the day off. We're not under any real time pressure.'

'I'm fine,' Samantha said quickly, avoiding the sympathetic look the old actor was giving her. There was such a warm, fatherly air about him that if she wasn't careful she would be unburdening herself to him. 'I didn't sleep very well,' she added. 'That's all.'

'As I vaguely recall,' Mark said, smiling in a slightly one-sided manner that reminded Samantha of Blaize, 'there is usually only one thing that leads a healthy young woman like you to lose sleep. What's his name?'

Samantha chewed her lip, feeling her cheeks grow warm. Drat! Why did she have to give herself away like that? Should she tell Mark about Blaize Leighton? She didn't want him to think that she was going to fall apart every time someone tried to pry some information out of her.

'It's just someone who's being a little too... persistent,' she replied. 'I think I may have got rid of him.'

'And you wish you hadn't,' Mark stated flatly. 'Are you sure all is lost?'

'No!' Samantha said sharply. That wasn't how she felt. Was it? 'I-I mean——' she stammered, realising her reply was not entirely appropriate in any case, and not sure how to explain her problem without revealing too much. 'I mean that I'm not sure whether he's really interested in me, and even if he is, he's not my type.'

Mark leaned back in his chair and shook his head, sipping his cup of coffee and eyeing Samantha thoughtfully.

'You know, Samantha,' he said finally, 'it seems to me that if I'm going to reveal all of my deeds and misdeeds to you, that you might as well share your problems with me. I have, after all, a few dozen years of experience to bring to bear on them. Now, why is it you don't know whether this young man is sincerely interested in you? Has he proved himself fickle in the past?'

Oh, dear, Samantha thought, now I *am* in trouble. I can't very well decline his offer of help without seeming terribly rude. She moistened her lips nervously. Well, she might as well tell him the truth. It usually proved the best course in the long run.

'It's nothing like that,' she answered. 'I know for a fact that when he first contacted me a large part of his motivation was curiosity about what you might have to say about his father in your book. Now he claims he's only interested in me, and that if he wants to discuss the other, he'll come to you. But I just can't believe he suddenly finds me that fascinating. He sends flowers every day. At least until today he did. And he's been calling every night. Since he went back to New York, that is. And . . .'

'Whoa!' said Mark Westland. 'You're overloading my memory. Start by telling me who the young man's father might be.'

'George Blaize Leighton,' Samantha replied. 'His son calls himself Blaize, but he's really G. B. Leighton, Jr. His father is dead, but, from what I gathered, his mother is the one who's concerned about what you might have to say. She's the keeper of the family image, I guess. Blaize was out here on business, and he saw us on the Findley show and decided to track me down after that.'

'Hmmm,' Mark said, rubbing the cleft in his chin with a characteristic gesture, all the while studying Samantha's face intently. 'Yes, I remember old George Leighton. I played poker with him a few times at a men's club in New York, back in the early fifties. He was a terrible poker player. The sorest loser I ever met. Couldn't hold his liquor worth a damn, either. One night, after I'd taken a couple of thousand from him in a game of show down, he took a swing at me on the sidewalk right in front of the Waldorf, for absolutely no reason that I could detect. I decked him with one punch.' The old actor's eyes twinkled. 'I was pretty scrappy in those days, and the press made the most of it. I should probably include that with some other stories of fights I should have stayed out of but didn't.'

Samantha frowned. 'There's certainly no point in letting someone take a swing at you for no reason. I wonder what he had in mind? Maybe Blaize's mother knows and is afraid you know something that you don't about his father.'

'Could be,' Mark said, 'and then it might also be that now that he's gone she wants his image to be absolutely without blemish. Some women are like that. If that's the case, I might leave him out. I'll reserve judgement until I see how you and his son get along. What's the boy like? You say you aren't compatible. Why? It's fairly obvious that his attentions are making quite an impression.'

'Well . . .' Samantha paused, feeling uncomfortably like a witness being interrogated. 'He's just such a...an incurable romantic,' she blurted. 'And he does such crazy things!' She went on to describe her brief relationship with Blaize Leighton, concluding crossly with, 'I don't see why you find it amusing,' as Mark chuckled over Blaize's instructions about his cards. 'You look just like he does when he's twisting what I've said around to suit his own purposes.'

'Maybe that's because he seems to do exactly what I'd do under the circumstances,' Mark replied. 'I think you'd better give the lad a chance. Don't sell yourself short. He may be telling the truth when he says his interest has shifted to you, and there's a lot to be said for roses and romance. Keep me informed on how things are going, will you?'

'I doubt they'll be going very well, if at all,' Samantha replied tightly. She might have guessed that Mark Westland would take Blaize's side. After all, what else should she expect from one of Hollywood's most famous romantic heroes?

'Now, now, Samantha, you remind me of...' Mark began and Samantha quickly turned on her recorder, thankful that he was now off on his own escapades and she could get her mind off of Blaize Leighton. The more she thought about him, the more confused she became.

By the time Samantha left for home, she had completely forgotten her earlier distress, so entranced had she been by Mark Westland's accounts of his early movies, the first as a song and dance man, the second that magical moment in his life when a famous producer's intuition and Mark's own grace and skill suddenly were combined in an historic role in which Mark wore a period costume and fought a duel over a beautiful woman, a role he was to repeat with variations throughout his long career.

'I've got to rent those movies and study them,' Samantha reminded herself again as she parked her car in front of her apartment. Maybe this weekend...

'Sam, you are not going to believe what has been going on!'

Before Samantha could even open her car door, Bill Grimes was there, gesturing agitatedly toward her apartment.

'What?' she asked, getting out of her car and staring in the direction of Bill's waving hand. 'I don't see anything.'

'Just look in your backyard,' Bill replied, following along as Samantha hurried toward her door. 'Is that

Leighton guy planning on moving in with you, or what?'

Baffled, Samantha could only give Bill a blank look before she opened her door and then followed him as he led the way to the glass doors in her kitchen.

'Good lord,' was all she could say when she saw what he had meant. Gone was the unsightly bare spot where the plumber's trench had been. The entire yard had been covered with new, emerald-green turf, upon which a sparkling sprinkler now played. Along the south fence, a row of rose-bushes bloomed. As if in a dream, Samantha pushed open the door and stepped outside, walking slowly around the edge of her little yard, pausing to look at the giant tuberous begonias spreading their spectacular blooms on the shady side, the potted camellias on her patio, a hibiscus bush in one back corner, a young orange tree in the other. Everything looked impossibly perfect, the whole small yard breathtakingly beautiful.

'Well?' Bill demanded as Samantha returned to his side and stood, silently staring at her yard, her hands knotted together, an almost unbearable tension building inside of her. Was all of this Blaize Leighton's doing? What on earth was the man thinking of?

'Well what?' she snapped back. 'I don't know anything about this! Who did it? Maybe they got the wrong place!'

'Oh, no,' Bill said, shaking his head. 'Your neighbour on the right called and said he could see a bunch of men tearing up your yard, and wondered if I knew anything about it. I came over to see what was going on, and it was a landscape gardening outfit with two trucks and six men. They had an order from a Mr Leighton to do all of this, and they'd taken your back gate off the hinges and gone right in. You mean he didn't ask you about doing it?'

Samantha shook her head, feeling strangely giddy. 'No. He didn't say a word about it. I guess ... I guess I shouldn't have told him I'd rather have a box of grass seed than any more plants.' She smiled weakly at Bill, who was staring at her in obvious disbelief. 'He did get a bit carried away, didn't he?'

'Carried away?' Bill roared. 'Carried away? My God, woman, have you any idea what this must have cost? There was a regular army working here.'

'Well, don't blame me! I didn't ask for it!' Samantha cried. 'Now, just leave me alone, will you? I've got to decide what to do about it.'

'What can you do? You can't very well roll up the sod and dig up the plants and send them back. I tell you, Samantha, that guy's really after you. You'd better decide if you want him before he tears down the building next door and puts up a church for you two to get married in!'

'Don't be ridiculous,' Samantha replied, but her voice carried little conviction. It wasn't too hard to imagine Blaize Leighton doing exactly that. She had better find some way to get her message through to him that this kind of nonsense found no favour with her before he tried it. When her telephone rang later that evening, she was still trying to find the way.

'Hello?' she answered, her taut nerves stretching another notch tighter.

'Hello, beautiful,' came those warm, deep tones. 'Are you feeling better today? I'm afraid I upset you last night.'

'Last night?' Samantha cried, the sound of Blaize's voice sending her head spinning in spite of everything she told herself about remaining calm and logical. She fought for control, but finally gave up and exploded loudly, 'I was not upset last night! I am upset today! What in God's name possessed you to redo my entire backyard? I only wanted a box of grass seed. Can't you ever listen to what I say? I said grass seed and I *meant* grass seed! I don't want to be under obligation to you for something that costs thousands of dollars. I don't like it. It only means that you want something from me and you don't care what it costs to get it! Well, as far as I'm concerned, Mr Blaize Leighton, you can have those men come and take it all away. I'm not for sale!'

With that she banged her receiver down and grabbed for a Kleenex to wipe away the tears that had started running down her cheeks. Drat that man! Maybe now he'd finally believe her when she told him she didn't want to be showered with romantic gifts. Maybe he'd even believe she didn't want to see him again! She had barely finished drying her eyes when the telephone rang again. For a moment she considered not answering it, but after the fourth ring knew she could not ignore it. After all, it might be someone else.

'Hello?' she croaked over the lump in her throat.

'Samantha, listen to me.' Blaize's voice sounded unusually severe. 'Try, if you can, to look at things from a different viewpoint for a minute. I am not trying to buy you. Forget that damned book, if it's still on your mind. I want to do things for you because pleasing you makes me happy. I strongly suspect that once you get used to the change in your yard, you're going to be very happy with it. Somehow, I thought a surprise might be fun, but I guess I forgot that your first response would be to put the wrong interpretation on it. Why don't you look at it again in the morning and see how you feel then? If you still don't like it, I'll have it returned to its original state.'

Samantha swallowed hard. 'It-it's not the way it looks that I don't like,' she said. 'You're still trying to twist my words around. What I don't like is you spending so much money on me. It isn't right. Even if you're only trying to please me, it still isn't right. There are a lot of people who need very simple things more than I need that fancy backyard. Instead of spending the money to change it back, send the money to a charity. That would make a lot more sense.'

Blaize chuckled. 'No, it wouldn't, but I think it would be better to show you why instead of telling you. That always works better with you crusading reporter types. We'll take a little side trip this weekend so you can see what I mean. Now, about this weekend...'

'No! Please, Blaize, just leave me alone,' Samantha said, feeling her upper lip bead with anxious perspiration. There was absolutely no way she was going to go out with Blaize Leighton again. He tied her into knots from three thousand miles away. Any closer and she'd become a pretzel!

'No, Samantha, I'm not going to leave you alone. What you need to do is get used to having me close.' Blaize's voice became soft and gentle. 'Remember what we were doing last night? Pretending to be together?'

Samantha remembered, only too well. That was what had kept her tossing and turning, and frayed her nerves to the breaking-point. 'Yes, but I don't want to...'

'Good,' Blaize interrupted. 'I think what you need right now is to put your head on my shoulder and have a good cry. You've got yourself all tied up in knots. Go ahead. I don't mind getting a little damp.'

'D-darn you!' Samantha choked out as suddenly the tears she had been holding in since last night began to stream down her cheeks. How did he know that she was close to tears? She didn't want to cry like this. She wanted to be in control of herself! Even worse, she felt as if she really wanted to have her head on Blaize's shoulder. The man was a blasted magician!

'That's better,' Blaize said softly. 'Now I'm going to give you a kiss and help dry your tears.' He paused and Samantha heard a little kissing sound. 'There. You'll feel better now. You should be able to get a lot of work done tonight. I'll call you again tomorrow. Goodnight, sweetheart.'

'Goodnight, Blaize,' Samantha said hoarsely. She hung up her telephone and took a deep breath, letting it out slowly. She did feel better, in a way. Some of the tension had gone, but that was mostly physical. Mentally, she assessed her situation as being more like someone bailing madly with a teacup on the deck of the Titanic, while the water rose inexorably around them. She would either have to get to a lifeboat soon, or be drowned, engulfed in flowers and a soft, warm voice that belonged to a man she hardly even knew.

CHAPTER FOUR

BILL GRIMES was at Samantha's apartment early the next morning.

'How do you like that?' he asked, tossing a sketch on to her breakfast table before helping himself to a cup of coffee and sitting down across from her.

Samantha picked up the sketch and studied it. The central figure was obviously herself, in caricature, climbing up an orange tree to escape the tendrils of a mass of pursuing flowers which already were entwining themselves around one of her legs. To the side was a man in a flowing, Dracula-style cape, grinning evilly and waving a magic wand. 'You'll never get away, my dear,' he was saying. She shuddered at the uncanny accuracy with which Bill had captured the exact way she was feeling.

'I think you've captured the essence of the situation,' she said drily. 'That doesn't quite capture Blaize Leighton, though, except in spirit. It looks more like Mark Westland with fangs.'

Bill shrugged. 'I've only seen him from a distance, remember? It's the best I could do from a quick impression. Maybe you'll let me get a better look at him next time he's around. I assume he is coming back?'

'You didn't have to remind me this early in the morning,' Samantha said, grimacing. 'He's coming back Saturday and has some idiotic idea of going to

Disneyland. Maybe I should call the police and tell them he's harassing me.'

'I'm sure they'd love to hear your complaint.' Bill turned on a falsetto voice. 'Oh, officer, please help me. I don't know what to do. A man is trying to overwhelm me with flowers and plants and a trip to Disneyland. Please let all those murderers alone and save me from this terrible fate.'

'You don't need to remind me how ridiculous it is, either,' Samantha grumbled.

'What I don't understand,' Bill said, 'is why you don't just tell Blaize Leighton to go to blazes? Either you don't really want him to, or, for the first time since I've known you, you've lost the power of speech.'

'I have *tried* to tell him!' Samantha said loudly. 'He doesn't listen. He just goes right on being...romantic. He seems to think that if he does it long enough I'll turn into a romantic, too.'

'Is he right?' Bill asked, raising his eyebrows.

'No!' Samantha said, so loudly this time that Bill put up his hands as if to defend himself.

'My, but we're testy this morning.' He turned his head as the doorbell rang. 'Time for your daily dose of foliage. Shall I get it?'

'Please do,' Samantha said, trying to ignore the anticipatory tingle that went through her and telling herself that the sensible thing was to take whatever it was and throw it in the bin.

'This is, I believe, a terrarium,' Bill said, returning with a large, snifter-shaped glass object filled with tiny plants, and setting it in front of Samantha.

'Oh, how lovely!' Samantha said, any previous thoughts of disposing of the object vanishing into thin air. All she could do was stare at the tiny garden, arranged with little hills and a miniature pathway, on which two delicate oriental figurines were standing. 'Grandma always wanted one of these,' she said dreamily, her eyes misty.

'You're losing ground, Sam,' Bill warned. 'Tomorrow may be the *coup de grâce*.'

'It will not!' she replied vehemently, scowling at him. 'I can't help it if I love plants.'

By the next morning, Samantha was wondering if Bill might have been right. She was finding it more difficult all the time to really dislike Blaize Leighton. She and Blaize had had a long talk the previous night, precipitated when she mentioned how her grandmother had always longed for such a terrarium as Blaize had sent. They had exchanged family information, and she felt she had finally learned some things about Blaize as a person. He had not really wanted to go into the family business, only doing so because he was expected to carry on the tradition. His first love had always been the theatre. He had also, however, insisted on playing his little game of pretending to be close. He had told Samantha he needed a kiss on the forehead because he had a headache. She had felt so near to complying that instead she had said, 'Oh, go and take some aspirin!' and hung up to the sounds of his laughter.

The florist's delivery van arrived as usual, the now familiar delivery man grinning as he handed her a long, white box and said, 'Looks like American Beauties today, Miss Bennet.'

Relieved that at least Bill was not present to make any comments, Samantha opened the box and took out the card, wondering what fanciful thing Blaize might have said this time. With the terrarium, he had invited her to imagine the two of them inside the glass enclosure, strolling down the tiny path. This time the message was more serious. Much more serious. 'To help renew my image, which I fear may be fading along with the other blooms. I'll renew it in person tomorrow. Until then, keep safe in my love. Blaize.'

Samantha dropped the card as if it had suddenly become hot as fire. Blaize was now claiming to love her? He was out of his mind! He didn't know her that well, even if he did seem to be able to see through her a lot of the time. He should realise that making such an impossible statement only made it more difficult for her to believe that he was more interested in her than Mark Westland's book. He probably couldn't remember her any better than he expected her to remember him after the brief times they had spent together.

She shut her eyes and tried to remember Blaize's face in detail. It *was* hard. She could remember his dark, curly hair and his warm, brown eyes with evenly arched brows above them, but her most vivid memory was of his mouth and chin, just before he had kissed her. She could see the wide mouth, the lower lip more full than the upper, the square chin with the slight cleft in it, but when she tried to put his whole face together, she had trouble, the image coming out some kind of mixture of a younger version of Mark, whom she had seen every day, and someone else with different hair and colouring. Maybe it was because he did look a little like Mark. That was the way Bill had seen him, and his eye for human faces was exceptional.

With a sigh, Samantha picked up the lovely roses and breathed in their scent. No, this was no *coup de grâce,* but it could be a symbol of a new problem. It was possible that Blaize had actually convinced himself that he was in love with her. If so, it was more imperative than ever that she get through that foggy wall of romance and roses and talk some sense into him before he got badly hurt. She was not about to let him use it as an emotional club to persuade her to do something she did not want to do, any more than she had with Bill. It was quite different from fending off a man whose chief objective, she had assumed, was trying to seduce her into compromising both her morals and her journalistic ethics.

Thank goodness for Mark Westland and his book, Samantha thought later as she sat down to work on her notes and tapes. If it weren't for him, she would have spent the entire day dithering over Blaize Leighton's return on the morrow. As it was, she had relived with Mark some of his grandest moments during the late thirties, when he became personally acquainted with the likes of Churchill and Roosevelt. Next week, he had promised, he would tell her of his war adventures. When Samantha had remarked that her research had led her to believe he'd spent the war behind a desk, he had grinned like a schoolboy. 'Disinformation,' he had said. 'I was in counter-intelligence.'

'What a life,' Blaize commented later when he called and Samantha told him a few of the facts. 'It makes me feel about as exciting as a peanut-butter sandwich next to veal parmigiani.'

He sounded so down-hearted that Samantha quickly said, 'I prefer peanut butter,' and then wished she hadn't. It was probably just one of quick-witted Blaize's traps.

'That's the nicest thing you ever said to me,' he said, the laughter in his voice confirming her suspicions.

'Don't get your hopes up. I meant the food, not your analogy,' Samantha replied, then wondered why she felt glad when Blaize laughed heartily and accused her of being a transparent liar. It was almost as if she wanted him to believe the opposite of what she said.

'That reminds me,' Blaize said next, 'you haven't commented on the card you got today. I thought you'd have a few thousand things to say about that. Did you keep it or throw it to the dogs?'

Samantha felt her hands grow clammy. She had hoped the subject wouldn't come up at all, for she still was not sure how to cope with Blaize's declaration of love. Now she had to think of something, fast. She cleared her throat to gain time.

'Samantha? Don't tell me it left you speechless,' Blaize teased gently.

'No. Actually, all it did was make me more suspicious than ever of both your motives and your sanity,' she replied. 'You couldn't possibly be in love with me. You don't know me that well.'

'You don't believe in love at first sight?'

'No, I certainly do not! It's not ... not sensible at all. I think it indicates a lack of maturity.' Samantha smiled to herself at that last ad lib, which seemed to have put a temporary hold on Blaize's conversation. Maybe that gave him some food for thought. At least he wasn't laughing.

'Samantha,' he said finally, 'I think you may be right. I think that part of me had never quite grown up before I met you, and found out what it's like to really love someone. Someone aside from family, that is. It's rather frightening, but I like it. You'll find out what I mean quite soon, I think.'

He had done it again, Samantha thought, shaking her head in dismay and staring at the telephone in her hand. He'd twisted her words around to suit his own purposes, paying no attention to the message she'd tried to convey.

'That's not what I meant, and you know it!' she cried. 'Why don't you go and read a good book on the use of the English language? I have to get back to work now.'

'All right, sweetheart,' Blaize said calmly. 'Just remember that I love you and I'll see you at about ten in the morning. Have the coffee ready. Goodnight, love.'

He hung up, leaving Samantha staring at the phone, trembling in sheer frustration. Too bad he hadn't invited her to unburden herself tonight. She would have let out a scream that would have deafened him! As the thought occurred to her, she did just that, and then clapped her hand over her mouth, shaking her head at her stupidity. She wasn't out in the country, she was sitting near an open window in the city. Now her dogs were barking and the neighbours would probably think she was being murdered. The telephone rang.

'Hello? Oh, hello, Mrs Holloway... No, I'm all right. Just having a spot of trouble with my writing.'

'Good lord, the man is driving me bonkers,' she muttered when her concerned neighbour had hung up. 'I think I'll take a cold shower. Or maybe just fill the tub and drown myself in bubbles.'

*   *   *

By morning, Samantha felt quite pleased with herself. It had cost her a lot of sleep, but she had managed to talk herself into a state of relative calm. Blaize was either being diabolically clever, hoping to use his declaration of love to play on her sympathies, or he actually did believe he loved her. Either way, it didn't make much difference. She was used to Bill hovering about, looking hopeful. There wasn't much else that Blaize Leighton could do, either, if she didn't encourage him, and she was not about to do that. She was going to put her foot down, too. No more flowers, no more crazy gifts, and even if he sat on her doorstep for ever, she was not going out with him.

She dressed in a white, tailored shirt and blue slacks, and plaited her hair into one long braid, in an effort to convey as businesslike and non-sexy an image as possible. After a cursory trip through her apartment with the duster, Samantha brewed the coffee and sat down to read the morning paper. She did not even start when her doorbell rang, and she followed her excited dogs to the door with only the mildest tingle of anticipation. She flung open the door, ready to say a simple hello. Instead, she stood there stunned, her heart accelerating like a racing car, and her head reeling as if she had been hit with a sudden blow.

'Miss Bennet, I wonder if I might have a word with you?' Blaize asked, smiling that crooked smile, his eyes so alive and warm that Samantha could feel their heat like a tangible force. 'I've brought you these...' He thrust a long, white box towards Samantha. 'May I come in?' When Samantha only stood before him, clutching the box, he cocked his head. 'Don't you recognise me?'

'Of course,' she got out in a choked voice. It was not a question of recognising him, it was a question of seeing him so differently from the first time he had stood there. This was not just a handsome, rather plastic creature. This was a tall, very sexy man, with slightly mussed hair, his beautiful suit a little rumpled from his long flight, in whose arms Samantha had lain and against whose broad shoulder she had cried. His blasted trick had worked! She felt as if she should fling herself into his arms and welcome him home. Instead, she stood stock still, afraid to move lest she do exactly that.

Without saying anything, Blaize moved inside and shut the door, removed the box from Samantha's numb fingers, and then took Samantha's hands in his.

'Is there anything you'd like to say before I kiss you,' he asked, deep smile lines crinkling from the corners of his eyes, 'besides "don't"?'

When Samantha only shook her head, he pulled her closer, one arm encircling her and his other hand very softly touching her cheek.

'You're so beautiful,' he murmured. 'I was almost afraid my memory was exaggerating, but it wasn't. It didn't do you justice. I did remember the exact shade of blue of your eyes, though.' He tipped her chin with his hand, smiled as his eyes roved over her face, then slowly moved his hand behind her neck and lowered his lips to meet hers.

The touch of Blaize's lips awoke Samantha from her trance like a bolt of lightning illuminating a dark summer night. What was she thinking of, standing here like a sleepwalker, letting Blaize Leighton do whatever he wanted?

'Don't!' she cried, pulling her head back and pushing her hands in between them. 'Let me go.'

For a moment, a trace of anger flickered in Blaize's eyes, but he quickly masked it with a crooked smile.

'That was a rather delayed reaction,' he said, tightening his grip in response to Samantha's attempts to wriggle free. 'Now that you have that out of your system, I *am* going to kiss you, so you might as well stop struggling. I may not be built like a football player, but I'm a lot stronger than you, and right now the desire for that kiss that I came three thousand miles for has given me the strength of ten.'

'I'll bite,' Samantha warned, but her voice was feeble. There was a dangerous glitter in Blaize's dark eyes that she had not anticipated, and it both frightened her and set her heart pounding erratically. With her eyes wide open and her mouth clamped tightly shut, she watched those soft lips come closer, those long-lashed eyes loom larger and larger.

I will not respond, I will not, she told herself over and over, her arms rigid between them. She felt a surge of electricity when Blaize's lips touched hers and gritted her teeth. His hands, softly caressing her back, felt wonderfully warm, but she did not care. It didn't matter that his lips were teasingly nibbling at the corners of her mouth, and that the brush of his cool cheek against hers felt like both fire and ice. What did she care if he smelled spicy and masculine, his arms around her strong and protective, his body lean and hard?

Blaize's hand crept into her hair, his lips pressed more insistently against hers. The electric shock became a steady, pulsing current that surged in rhythm to Samantha's pounding heart. Her eyes closed. It was so tiring to fight. Her arms ached from the effort. It would be so much nicer to stretch them up around his neck...there, that felt better. His mouth was so soft, his tongue so sweet. When had she opened her own lips?

With a deep sigh, Samantha leaned her full weight against Blaize. Her mouth opened to the urging of his tongue, and she trembled at the wild sensations of desire that enveloped her. Lights flickered and flamed behind her closed eyelids, while from her throat came small sounds of pleasure at the touch of Blaize's hands upon her breasts. She tightened her grip, her fingers plunging deep into his thick, dark curls. The world had stopped interfering with her pleasure, and she did not care. She only wanted this kiss to go on and on, until the desire that was flooding her knew no bounds. Could they go on like this, the excitement building ever higher, their clothing somehow disappearing, their bodies melting together and making their bond complete? That would be like the most perfect dream of how a man and woman should...

What am I thinking of? A sudden, cold shock hit Samantha as her imagination carried on her thoughts in vivid imagery.

'Stop!' she said hoarsely, pulling away with all of her strength. To her surprise, Blaize slowly released her, his eyes dark and filled with desire, but smiling at her with a velvety softness that seemed to wrap her in a cloak of warmth.

'I think that was about as far as we could go standing up,' he said, his lips joining his eyes in their smile. 'We'll have to try it somewhere more comfortable later.'

'We will not!' Samantha cried, jerking herself completely free. How could she have been so foolish as to lead him to think she was his for the asking? Especially when what she wanted him to think was that he had better seek female companionship elsewhere! 'I do not do that sort of thing, with you or anyone else, no matter how many flowers they bring me!' Her eyes fell on the box Blaize had just brought. 'I already have more than enough flowers,' she said, pointing to the box, 'so you can take those away and find someone else to give them to. This place is beginning to look like the setting for someone's funeral, and it is definitely not going to be mine! I knew all along there was just one thing you were really after. Talking about love doesn't fool me. I wasn't...'

Samantha was about to say 'born yesterday', but suddenly she found herself back in Blaize's arms, his hand clamped firmly over her mouth.

'Enough!' Blaize roared, his eyes sending a shower of angry sparks towards Samantha, then quickly becoming sparkling with mirth instead. 'I am not trying to seduce you. I was merely responding to what I felt coming from you. I do love you, or I wouldn't put up with your nonsense. Remember that old cliché, "you're beautiful when you're angry"? Well, you are. Your cheeks get as red as roses. Now, let's declare a truce. Is the coffee ready? I need some. I've been up since five a.m. and I need something to bolster me before we trek out to Disneyland.'

'I'm not ready for a truce,' Samantha said as soon as Blaize removed his hand, for an idea had occurred to her while he was talking, and she could hardly wait to try out its effects. She would not argue with him about Disneyland, she would simply detour him to something she felt was more worth while. It would doubtless be very revealing to watch him squirm in discomfort.

'I just thought of the perfect thing to do with my surfeit of flowers,' she went on. 'We're going to pack them all up and take them to the Shady Oaks Rest Home. That's the rest home where my grandmother lived her last years. I still go there to visit quite often, and believe me, those people need something to brighten their lives a lot more than I do.'

Blaize's forehead puckered into a frown. 'We could easily have some flowers sent there,' he said. 'I'm sure the florist would be glad for the extra business.'

'No!' said Samantha, scowling. She waved her hand towards her bouquets. 'We take these!'

'All right,' Blaize said with a sigh. 'But can I have some coffee first? Please?' He smiled beguilingly.

'I guess so.' Samantha smiled also, but hers was a smile of pleasure that her idea had worked so well. A trip to Shady Oaks was the ideal way to demonstrate to Blaize Leighton that she and he were not on the same wavelength at all. Not only that, but it might open his eyes to some of the problems that money alone couldn't solve. He was going to learn something he hadn't bargained for when he had first come knocking on her door.

'You don't want to take your terrarium, do you?' Blaize asked a short time later, his need for coffee fulfilled.

Samantha paused only a moment in her wrapping of the flowers for transport.

'Yes, I do,' she replied. This whole exercise would be meaningless if it appeared that she wouldn't part with anything she really wanted herself.

'All right,' Blaize said, giving Samantha a sceptical look. 'I'm not sure what you're trying to prove, but I can see you're determined to have your own way at the moment. Be forewarned, though, I'll just get you another one, and there will be more flowers for you. You love them, and you should have them.'

'If I want them, I'll get them myself,' she said, frowning. 'There. I think everything's ready.'

With the flowers safely packed into the back seat of Blaize's Mercedes, Samantha proceeded to give Blaize directions to the rest home, which was located in a rather run-down neighbourhood in an industrial section of Los Angeles.

'I guess I should warn you that Shady Oaks is not the kind of place you'd be likely to send your mother to,' she said, 'but it was the best I could afford when my grandmother was alive, and it's all any of the other patients can afford today. I'm planning on using any money I get from Mark Westland's memoirs to help buy some things they need.'

'That's very admirable,' Blaize said, glancing over at her and smiling. 'However, I don't think you should feel guilty because you couldn't provide something more elegant for your grandmother. I'm sure she knew you were doing the best you could, and appreciated it very much.'

'That's not the point!' Samantha took a deep breath and counted to ten to squelch her irritation. 'I don't feel guilty, I feel responsible. I think elderly people deserve more than having some faceless bureaucracy handing them a pittance, and a shabby home that provides minimal care. Maybe you'll see what I mean when you meet some of the people.'

'I though we were delivering flowers, not paying a visit,' Blaize said, frowning.

'Well, you thought wrong,' Samantha replied, inwardly delighted that Blaize apparently found the idea unsettling. Not that she wouldn't have expected it. It wasn't quite like a trip to Disneyland.

When they stopped in the circular drive in front of the rambling, one-storey structure, Blaize still seemed uneasy.

'I may as well tell you,' he said, gathering up an armload of flowers, 'that visiting with sick people makes me uncomfortable. I never know what to say,'

Taking a little pity on him, Samantha patted his arm.

'Most people don't. But these people aren't really sick, most of them are only suffering from fairly normal problems of old age that made it impossible for them to live alone any longer. Some are here because their families couldn't take them, some because they didn't want to inconvenience their families. Just try to talk to them as if they're part of your family. Show a little interest in them. That's all you need to do.'

The staff all greeted Samantha warmly, bubbling with enthusiam over the flowers and dispatching an aide to come up with some containers for them.

'It may have to be old coffee cans,' the head nurse said with a wry smile, 'but we'll find enough somehow.' She looked hopefully at Blaize. 'Maybe you could take a bouquet to Mrs McCarthy. She's been feeling terribly down this week. She refuses to leave her room. Last Tuesday was her birthday, and she didn't even get a card from her son.'

'Oh, no!' Samantha cried, her own heart immediately saddened. 'You'll love Mrs McCarthy,' she said, looking entreatingly at Blaize. 'She was an actress in silent films. Usually she's so perky.'

Blaize looked doubtful, but he smiled briefly at Samantha and the nurse.

'I'll see what I can do,' he said.

Samantha led Blaize through the corridors, taking the opportunity to point out to him their need of paint. She paused at the door, gave Blaize an encouraging smile, and then opened it a little.

'Hello, Mrs McCarthy,' she said, poking her head inside. 'It's Samantha Bennet. May I come in? I've brought a friend who'd like to meet you.'

'Oh, hello, dear,' came a feeble voice from deep in a pile of pillows. 'I don't know if I'm fit to see anyone. I haven't been up to snuff this week.'

'Sure you are,' Samantha replied, going inside and leading Blaize in after her. 'We're here to get you back up to snuff.' She smiled down at the tiny old woman. 'Shall we raise you up a little so you can see this handsome man I've brought to visit?'

'Oh, my!' said the old woman, immediately smiling a shy smile as she saw Blaize, leaning over Samantha's shoulder. 'He is a nice-looking boy, isn't he? Is he your sweetheart?'

Before Samantha could reply, Blaize stepped forward, bouquet in hand.

'She's trying for the title,' he replied gallantly, 'but now that I've seen you, I'm not sure she'll get it, and I definitely think that you're the one these roses belong to. Happy Birthday. I'm sorry I'm a little late.' So saying he handed the flowers to Mrs McCarthy and then leaned over and planted a kiss on her wrinkled cheek.

'Roses!' Mrs McCarthy breathed, flushed with pleasure. 'How long it's been since I had any roses. My husband always sent me roses on my birthday. Roses mean love, he always said, God rest his soul. He was such a romantic man. I always felt sorry for the women I knew who got practical gifts instead of flowers or perfume from their husbands. Yes, raise me up, Samantha, and let me get a better look at this young man of yours. Better, yet, introduce me to him. If I'm going to steal him from you, I need to know his name.

Samantha quickly went to turn the crank at the end of the bed, but her eyes remained glued to Blaize's face. He was giving his full attention and a warm smile to the old woman, who insisted he was to call her Amanda and who was talking away a mile a minute in response to his tactful questions. Was this the man who was afraid he might not know what to say?

Quietly, Samantha stole away to find a container for the flowers. Chalk one up for Blaize Leighton, she thought wryly. He had certainly risen to the occasion. The next question was how he would feel about the experience once they had left the home. Would he sigh in relief that it was over, or wish he could come back again?

It was several hours before she was to find out her answer, for Blaize went from one of the elderly patients to another, having lunch in the bare little dining-room with those who were ambulatory, and seeming loath to leave at all. The ladies, especially, responded to his elegant manners and gallant remarks, a sparkle of what had once been youthful beauty returning to their eyes. More than once, Samantha found her eyes misty at the joy with which the simple gift of a few flowers was received, and several times she noticed Blaize blinking with suspicious rapidity.

When he had finished talking to the patients, Blaize spent almost half an hour talking to Robert Patterson, the administrator of the home, a man whom Samantha had always found standoffish. With Blaize, the man seemed positively jovial, pumping Blaize's hand enthusiastically as he took his leave.

When they got back into the car, Blaize sat for several minutes, staring straight ahead and saying nothing, his jaw clenched so tightly that the muscles in his cheeks stood out. Samantha felt her spirits sink. As time wore on, she had begun to feel that she had greatly understimated Blaize Leighton, and begun hoping against hope that she might convince him to come again. Now it seemed he might have found the experience so trying that he did not know how to express his unhappiness. Unwilling to ask and find out the worst, Samantha sat quietly, her hands clenched in her lap. At last Blaize spoke, still looking straight ahead.

'I told Patterson to put together a bill of particulars of what the home needs and I'd see that the Leighton Foundation sent them some funds.'

'Why, Blaize, that's . . . wonderful,' Samantha said quickly. It wasn't quite what she had hoped for, but it would certainly help. She was totally unprepared when suddenly he turned and looked at her, his expression dark with anger.

'That is what you wanted, isn't it?' he said harshly.

Samantha stared at him in horror, tears springing to her eyes. Was that what he thought? That she had only brought him here because of his money?

'Good lord, no!' she cried. 'I never even thought of that!'

'Then why?' Blaize asked, his expression softening a little at the sight of Samantha dashing the tears from her cheeks with an impatient hand. 'Here,' he said gruffly, handing her a snowy handkerchief.

'Because,' Samantha said, sniffing and mopping her tears at the same time, 'I wanted to show you that there are people who need things a lot more basic than romantic dinners and roses. I wanted you to see that those things are a silly waste of time and money, but I didn't mean to make you feel obliged to give money to the home. Anyway, I guess, in a way, I was wrong.'

'Oh?' Blaize lifted one eyebrow and waited while Samantha blew her nose vigorously. 'So you thought I needed to be taught a lesson. And exactly what do you mean by your amazing semi-admission that you might have been wrong?'

Samantha flushed uncomfortably and looked down at her hands. 'I mean,' she said huskily, 'that that's exactly what all of the ladies were longing for. Something to remind them of when they were young, when the men they loved brought them roses and took them out for romantic evenings. That meant more to them than anything money could buy.' She looked back at Blaize. 'They really liked you. You seemed to know just what to say. What I wanted...was hoping...was that you'd be willing to come and see them again sometimes.'

'Samantha, Samantha,' Blaize said, shaking his head and smiling at her in amazement, 'did you really think that I don't know what the world is all about? Of course I'll come back, even though I find it difficult because it almost breaks my heart. I think that you're the one who needs to learn another lesson or two.'

'What lessons are those?' Samantha asked apprehensively. She was beginning to feel very strongly that there was a lot more to Blaize than she had suspected, and that if he felt like paying her back with a lesson of his own, it could be quite surprising, if not frightening.

'Number one,' Blaize said as he finally started the car, 'may take a while, although I think we've made a start. That is to convince you that there are more things in life than crusades and causes, and that you needn't feel guilty for enjoying them. This is one of those things.' He suddenly leaned over and kissed Samantha firmly on the mouth. 'The other thing,' he added, grinning at her surprised stare, 'I'll show you in a short while. Remember the other night I told you there was something I needed to show you?'

'You mean something to do with landscaping my yard?'

Blaize nodded. 'It's not far from here.'

He drove through an area even more depressingly run-down than where the home was located. Suddenly, just past a row of abandoned buildings, he turned. There, in a large area from which all of the old buildings had been cleared, they came upon a most unlikely sight. Row upon row of young green shrubs and trees were growing. There were sprinklers playing upon newly planted seedlings. Lattices protected an assortment of more delicate plants and flowers. In the middle of the block, a large greenhouse stood behind a smaller white building upon which the words 'Plants Unlimited' were painted in bright colours.

'This,' said Blaize, 'is the source of some of the materials used in landscaping your yard. There is also a sod farm which supplied your new grass, and a strictly florist business, from which all of your roses and plants have come. And it all belongs to six inner-city boys who had the idea and brought their proposal to the Leighton Foundation about five years ago. Come on in and meet Joe Newsome. He runs this part of the business.'

Samantha got out and followed Blaize, thinking that now she knew what people meant when they said they felt about two feet tall. He must think she was a real idiot for believing him to be so stupid and vacuous that he neither knew nor cared about those less fortunate than himself. Still, she didn't quite understand how you could care so deeply one minute and the next act as if the problem didn't even exist. Apparently, Blaize thought she ought to learn how to do just that. Why? Why couldn't he take her the way she was? Still brooding over that question, she met the enthusiastic young man Blaize had mentioned and tried to make the appropriate responses as he told her some details of how he and his friends had started their business and made it grow as beautifully as their plants.

'Something's bothering you,' Blaize said as they again returned to his car. 'Come on, out with it.'

Blaize's perceptiveness only compounded Samantha's distress. Where on earth did he get his knack for seeing inside her head?

'I feel like a fool, and yet I don't,' Samantha replied, after deciding that there was no more literate way she could describe her emotions. 'I feel stupid for thinking you were insensitive to a lot of social problems, and yet I can't see why there's anything wrong with the way I am. Maybe I don't want your lesson in how to ignore things I don't want to see when it suits me.'

'That's not quite the way it works, my love,' Blaize said, leaning over and giving Samantha another kiss as he started the car. 'That's why you need lessons. Now, in case you hadn't noticed, it has been about ten years since lunch. I don't know about you, but I'm starved. How about some hamburgers? Then we can go back to your place and snuggle up on the nice soft sofa of yours while you tell me the rest of the story of your life.'

'The hamburgers sound good,' Samantha replied warily. At least she wasn't going to be asked to dress formally and drink champagne this evening. She was not about to be tricked into agreeing with Blaize's second proposal. She already seemed to have lost control of this day, which was not going at all as she had planned. Snuggling on the sofa with Blaize would really put the finishing touches on it . . . the first wave over the bow of her sinking Titanic.

Blaize chuckled. 'Still have your guard up, don't you? Well, I won't force you to snuggle if you don't want to, although I think it would be good for you. Tomorrow morning, however, there is definitely something we are going to do.'

'What is that?' Samantha asked.

'We are going to Disneyland.'

CHAPTER FIVE

SAMANTHA opened her mouth to protest and then closed it. After all that Blaize had done today it would be terribly ungrateful of her to argue about that project, although why he was so insistent about it she couldn't fathom.

'Why is it you're so determined to take me to Disneyland?' she asked.

Blaize shrugged. 'I guess because it's one of my favourite places, and it's more fun to go with someone who hasn't really seen it.'

'Hasn't really...Blaize, I've been there dozens of times!' Samantha cried. 'I used to live only five miles from there. It was fun when I was younger, but I've outgrown it.'

'No, you haven't. You just think you have,' Blaize replied. 'That's why I said you haven't really seen it.'

'Another lesson,' Samantha muttered, mostly to herself, staring glumly out the window. How was it the role of teacher and pupil that she had planned had got so completely reversed? She turned her head at the sound of a low chuckle from Blaize. He glanced over at her and smiled.

'I'm afraid I'm going to have to insist on that snuggle later, after all. You've got yourself in a terrible funk just because things aren't going the way you planned them.'

'I have not!' Samantha denied hotly, although Blaize, as usual, had put his finger right on the problem. Maybe if he'd stop picking her psyche apart she'd be in a better humour. 'And I certainly can't see how snuggling, as you call it, can serve any purpose that I might have in mind,' she added, scowling. She could feel every muscle in her body tense at the images that verb conjured.

'Depends on what you're thinking of,' Blaize said, his eyes twinkling mischievously. 'However, if you're worried that it's a plot I have to try and sneak up on sex, don't be. You *are* in a funk, no matter what you say, and I think you badly need to learn to be close and warm and find out what it's like to trust someone, instead of always putting both physical and intellectual distance in the way. If we'd had time to do that before today you wouldn't have made the mistake about me that you did.'

'What mistake?' Samantha asked defensively, although she knew perfectly well that she had made several.

'You'd planned to have me shown up for a callous, inept hedonist who couldn't cope with the darker side of life by now, and had already mentally disposed of me several times. It's not much fun to have a grand theory like that demolished. You're willing to admit that you're wrong, but you aren't ready to really believe it yet. That might be the beginning of admitting to yourself that you love me.'

'How can I admit what isn't so?' Samantha asked, her voice rising with frustration. Wasn't there any way to discourage Blaize's determined pursuit of her? 'Look, Blaize,' she said, trying another tactic, 'I've admitted that you're a much better person than I thought at first. I think you should be satisfied with that. I'm not in love with you now, and I'm not going to be later. What will it take to convince you of that?'

'After what happens when we kiss, nothing would,' Blaize replied. 'However, lest you think I'm basing all of my predictions on a physical response, I am not. We're so similar in many ways that it's uncanny.'

'Similar? That's the wildest idea I've heard yet!' Samantha said, shaking her head. She stared at the outline of Blaize's neatly chiseled profile and suddenly he turned his head and gave her a seductive wink.

'How else do you think I'm able to understand you so well, my love?' he asked, with his voice pitched extra low and a devilish smile on his face. That smile, combined with the wink and the voice, made him seem far too much like Bill's caricature of him to suit her.

'Then why don't I understand you?' Samantha complained, frowning.

'When you stop being afraid of love, you will,' Blaize said confidently.

It was early evening when they finally arrived back at Samantha's apartment, Samantha having delayed as long as she could by insisting she needed to go to the grocer's and stop and pick up her cleaning, after they had finished a dinner as leisurely as she could make it at a fast-food restaurant. The idea of snuggling on the couch with Blaize had her nerves so taut that she was on the verge of letting out another blood-curdling shriek to relieve the tension. Could she really trust him? Could she trust herself? Finally, she could delay no longer. The groceries had been put away, the dogs fed, and Blaize had put some records on her stereo and turned the lights down low. Jacket and tie and shoes off, and his shirt unbuttoned almost to the waist, he was stretched out comfortably on her sofa, watching Samantha fiddle with straightening a pile of magazines.

'I think you've stalled as long as I'm going to let you,' he said softly, beckoning with one finger. 'Come here, Samantha.'

'Er—maybe I should put on something more comfortable,' she said, jerking to attention, her hands clenched together before her.

Blaize laughed. 'All right. How about that caftan you had on the night I fell in the trench? Don't take your hair out of that braid, though. I want to do that myself. I've been thinking about it all day.'

Without making any reply, Samantha fled up the stairs and into her room. She eyed the door which opened on to the little deck above her patio speculatively. Maybe she should climb down the bougainvillaea vine and run away. She could be miles away before Blaize suspected anything. She sighed. It would never work. The vine would probably break and she'd fall and end up in the hospital, although at the moment that didn't sound like too bad an option. But there would still be tomorrow, and the day after, and the day after that, and she couldn't keep running for ever. With Blaize's persistence, that was how long she would have to run.

Reluctantly she stripped off her shirt and slacks and put on the long caftan, her mind refusing to confront the question of why she was doing what Blaize asked if it frightened her so, even though she asked herself the question directly as she peered in the mirror. Maybe, she thought wryly, she should ask Blaize. He seemed to have all the answers.

'Ah, there you are at last,' Blaize said, smiling as Samantha returned to her living-room, her feet having performed the act of taking her there without her actually commanding them to. He moved against the back of the couch and patted the space beside him. 'Come and sit down.'

Samantha sat down stiffly and looked down at Blaize, trying to still her pounding heart. There was nothing really frightening about the man, she told herself. He had the warmest brown eyes and the gentlest smile she'd ever seen. She liked the way his brows arched so evenly. They were very expressive, but not bushy or pointy as some men's were. His bone structure was nice, too, even and rather classical. His mouth was a little wide, but she preferred that to one that was too small. All in all, there wasn't much to fault in his appearance.

'Have you decided you can stand to look at me?' Blaize asked, his slanted smile quirking upwards.

'I've seen worse,' Samantha replied, cursing the blush she felt rise to her cheeks. She might as well be naked, she was so transparent to this man.

'Thank you,' Blaize said drily, although his eyes were alight with something between mischief and sheer devilry. 'Now turn your head so I can take the elastic off of your braid.'

'Don't pull my hair,' Samantha warned. 'I'll scream.'

'There,' Blaize said a moment later. 'Now, lie down and put your head on my shoulder.'

Samantha looked back at him and frowned. 'Somehow, I don't think this is going to work out, with you giving me instructions like some kind of robot. Besides, I'm still not sure I trust you.' She let out a little squeal, as Blaize suddenly grabbed her and put her into the position he had suggested.

'Anything to please milady,' he said, his mouth only inches from Samantha's. 'And you can trust me,' he said, his smile warm, but the expression in his dark eyes more serious than seductive. 'The question is, can I trust you?'

'I...' Samantha swallowed what felt like a lump the size of a tennis ball in her throat, her cheeks burning at the recognition of the longings that were making themselves insistenly know at the touch of Blaize's body against hers. 'Of course you can,' she said hoarsely.

'Good,' Blaize said. He smoothed her cheek with a cool hand. 'Don't look so worried. Just because we agree that nothing is going to happen doesn't mean we won't feel anything,' he said softly. 'It means that we begin to learn that those feelings are only a small part of something more important. Do you understand what I'm trying to say?'

'I think so,' Samantha replied, although lying there, staring into Blaize's beautiful dark eyes, she was not sure her mind was working at all. 'Something like love and sex aren't the same thing?'

'Exactly,' Blaize said, nodding approvingly.

'But I already knew that,' Samantha said. She certainly didn't need this kind of high-risk torture to teach her that lesson.

'Not really,' Blaize contradicted. 'You only know it as a platitiude you've heard others mouth. You've never felt it. You don't know that if you could get past the feelings of physical attraction for me, which I doubt even you will deny that you have, that there are many other kinds of warm, good things we can share and talk about. And if all you do is panic and run every time you feel sexual desire, you never will know. Of course, we could spend years trying to get past that barrier, but I'm not patient enough for that.'

'Oh,' was all that Samantha could think to say. She had never thought about it that way, and she had certainly never met a man who expressed it so directly. Whether it would work the way that Blaize planned, she was not so sure. She still felt as if she were wired for enough voltage to light a Christmas tree, every place that her body touched Blaize seeming to send fresh pulses of the current every few seconds. She shifted awkwardly as he put his hand behind her head and loosened her braid. Then he lifted her head and combed his fingers through her hair, spreading it out behind her. 'That looks beautiful,' he said, raising his head a little to admire it. He cuddled her head against his shoulder, tucked his other arm around to pull her close, and then nestled his lips against her forehead and kissed her softly. 'Now, just relax and tell me the story of Samantha when she was a little girl.'

'I can't remember if I ever was one,' Samantha said weakly. Her body felt as if it had turned to a quivering mass of jelly and was about to melt into the hard, male body beside her. She could feel the vibrations in Blaize's chest, as well as hear his roar of laughter at her statement.

'Maybe I'll have to prompt my little robot,' he said, the warmth of laughter still edging his deep voice. 'First, put your arm around me.' He lifted her arm and put it beneath his. 'Let's see. You were born...'

'In Bakersfield, California, on a Christmas Eve. The only daughter of Walter L. and Jane W. Bennet.'

'Very good,' Blaize said, giving her a squeeze. 'How long did you live there?'

'Until I was ten. Then I came to live with my grandparents in Long Beach.'

With prompting that became less and less necessary, Samantha told Blaize the story of her mother's struggle to make ends meet after her father died, the decision to send her to live with her grandparents when she was ten. There, things were easier. During high school, she worked on the school newspaper and decided to become a journalist. She had just started college when her grandfather died. His terminal illness had taken most of the old couples' savings, and Samantha took on the role of provider for her grandmother, managing to work and go to school at the same time, and keep her grandmother in her own home for several years. But finally she could no longer take care of things by herself, and Samantha was forced to make the unhappy decision to take her to Shady Oaks, a decision about which, she admitted, she probably did still feel a little guilty.

'If only it had all happened a couple of years later,' she said sadly. 'I had some lucky breaks after I quit the newspaper and started free-lancing. I could have afforded better then.'

'But then,' Blaize pointed out, 'the people at Shady Oaks wouldn't have had you for their champion. Maybe it's all for the best.'

'Said Dr Pangloss,' Samantha teased. 'Now it's your turn. The story of your life, if you please.'

'A spoiled rich brat, doted on by my mother and ignored by my father about sums it up,' Blaize said wryly. 'They were as unlike as night and day. My mother loved the theatre and music and exciting parties. And beauty of all kinds, flowers, especially. I always wondered why they ever married, and she told me after my father died that it was expected, just as I was expected to go into the family business. She said she'd often wished she'd kicked up her heels and married some romantic fellow she knew before my father, even though her family would have disowned her if she had.'

'Do I detect a slightly heavy-handed lesson in there somewhere?' Samantha asked, brushing a dark curl back from Blaize's forehead. As they had talked, she had gradually lost her terrible feeling of tension, finding that when Blaize said he wanted to snuggle he meant exactly that, nothing more. They had shifted positions and adjusted their bodies to each other many times, their touches unselfconscious, Blaize's little kisses undemanding.

'Could be,' Blaize replied with a grin, holding very still as Samantha's finger paused just above the cleft in his chin. 'Go ahead, you can touch it,' he said.

Samantha did, briefly, feeling a little awkward about it. 'Mark Westland has a cleft in his chin, too, only it's deeper than yours,' she explained. 'I always thought it must be hard to shave.'

'If it's deeper than mine, it is,' Blaize replied, taking Samantha's hand in his and rubbing her finger over his slightly rough chin. 'Were you suggesting I need to shave?'

'No,' Samantha replied, her eyes wandering over Blaize's chin and cheeks, which did show a tinge of darkness now. He was one of those men who looked attractive with a hint of stubble. She found her eyes lingering on his lips, and tension returned with a sudden jolt.

'Are you getting thirsty?' she asked, pushing herself quickly to a sitting position. 'I am.'

'I wouldn't mind a beer,' Blaize replied, 'and then I probably should be leaving. It's almost midnight.'

'I didn't realise it was so late,' Samantha said, feeling a chill as she got up and felt the coolness of the room away from Blaize's arms. She had just opened her refrigerator when her telephone rang. 'Who would call this late?' she wondered aloud as she went to answer it. Blaize, who had followed her, shrugged and raised his eyebrows expressively. 'Hello?' she said, putting the receiver to her ear.

'Miss Bennet,' said a harsh voice, 'this is William P. Lockwood. I want you to listen and listen well. If there is so much as a mention of my name in that book of Mark Westland's, there will be hell to pay, and both you and that old devil will pay it. I am a respected citizen of this state, and I won't have a few boyish pranks ruining my reputation. I can see to it that you can't get a job from here to Moscow, that's how much power I have. So pay attention, young lady. You hear?'

As the man ranted on, Samantha felt a cold fury rising inside her. What was this idiot doing, ruining her lovely evening with his insulting drivel?

'How dare you threaten me?' she shouted into the receiver when he paused, hoping she had deafened the man. 'You'll get exactly what you deserve in the book! No more and no less!'

'Yeah? Well, maybe I just ought to come over there and persuade you otherwise,' the man replied menacingly.

'Don't try it,' Samantha snapped and banged down the receiver, trembling with anger.

'Don't try what?' Blaize asked, grabbing her shoulders and turning her to face him, his expression serious and intent. 'Did someone threaten your life?'

'No, I don't think so,' she replied, trying to look unconcerned in the face of Blaize's worried frown. 'It was just some man who's afraid Mark will ruin his phoney image, and when I told him it wouldn't do any good to threaten me he said maybe he ought to come over here and persuade me otherwise. I think he was drunk.'

'Did he give his name?'

'Very positively. He seemed to think it would impress me. It was William P. Lockwood.' Samantha felt a shudder of apprehension at the dark look that came over Blaize's face at the mention of the man's name. 'Who is he?' she demanded.

'A major league crook,' Blaize replied. 'He's under congressional investigation for some money-laundering schemes. He's no one you want to fool with. You'd better come to my place in Malibu for the night. Tomorrow, I suggest you get in touch with Westland and have him call Lockwood and tell him he won't be mentioned. There's no point in risking your life for that book.'

Samantha frowned. 'No, Blaize,' she said. 'I'm not going to back off and I won't tell Mark to, either. I've had threats before on some of my investigative work. It's part of the business. I can take care of myself.'

'With a baseball bat?' Blaize shook his head. 'Samantha, this is serious. Come home with me now. Bring your dogs. Please. I care too much for you to let you take a chance.'

'No,' Samantha said again. 'I will not be frightened out of my own home.' She watched Blaize's mobile face go from angry to thoughtful, to almost pleased. 'Now what are you cooking up in that devious mind of yours?' she asked.

Blaize grinned. 'I think you're learning,' he said. 'I'm staying here tonight, my love. Don't argue, because it won't do you any good.'

'But . . . I don't have an extra bed,' Samantha said, blushing as Blaize laughed.

'I'll take the sofa,' he said, giving her shoulders a little squeeze. 'I've grown quite used to it already. I don't think you're quite ready for anything else. And,' he added as Samantha opened her mouth to speak, 'you needn't say you never will be. You will, and you know it.'

Samantha glared, but said nothing except, 'I'll get you some sheets and a blanket,' and walked away. Was it possible that this Lockwood person was someone Blaize had put up to making that call so that he could stay with her tonight? She wouldn't put it past him!

After fixing up her sofa for a bed for Blaize, Samantha followed him while he made a careful check of her doors, including the one in her bedroom, which he insisted on blocking with a heavy chest when he found how flimsy the lock was.

'There, that should do it,' he said, glancing at Samantha, who was watching him and wondering uncomfortably why she found it so reassuring to have him fussing over her, when for years she had hated the thought of anyone interfering in her independent style of life. He looked past her to her bed and smiled teasingly. 'Of course, if you'd let me stay up here, that wouldn't have been necessary.'

'Why, are you bullet-proof?' she asked sarcastically. Having Blaize so close to her bed had generated some rather disturbing images of further snuggling beneath the blankets that she would rather he didn't know about.

'Not entirely,' he replied. 'I have a scar in a very embarrassing place that I got in a hunting accident when I was fourteen.' He patted his left buttock and grinned. 'I'll show you some time soon.' He came close to Samantha and laid his hand on her cheek, smiling gently, in spite of the frown she was giving him. 'Now, lovely one,' he said, 'I must bid you goodnight with only a brotherly kiss, for if I do anything more there will definitely be two of us in that bed. Leave your door open, so I can hear if you call me.' He swiftly kissed her cheek. 'Goodnight, Samantha. I love you,' he said softly, then turned and left the room.

'Goodnight, Blaize,' Samantha murmured. She stood stock still, listening to the sounds of him going downstairs and then getting settled on her sofa, the patter of her dogs' feet as they followed this stranger in their midst telling her exactly where he was. She could picture his dark head against the snowy pillow, his lashes fanning out beneath his closed eyes. Somehow, it didn't seem strange at all that he should be there, her protector for the night. It gave her a warm feeling that had nothing to do with the deep, persistent physical longings she felt when he was near. Could he be right? Could she be falling in love with him?

With a sigh, Samantha turned and got into her bed. She wasn't sure. She wasn't sure of anything when Blaize was near, except that he could make her more unsettled than any other man in the world. She pulled her blankets tightly around her and tried not to think of snuggling next to someone warm and strong, nor of that mysterious scar that seemed unreasonably tantalising to imagine. Her sleepy mind ignored her efforts, and she faded into a world of dreams in which Blaize's arms held her close. It was a deep, blissful sleep, from which she partially awakened in the morning light, only to turn over and drift off again. Then, suddenly it was shattered by the sound of her dogs' raucous barking, men's voices cursing, and the crash of breaking glass.

'Good lord, what's going on?' she cried, instantly springing from her bed and grabbing her robe. Struggling to put it on, she ran to peer over the balcony into her living-room below.

'Oh, no! Stop that!' she screamed.

Bill Grimes, his face contorted with fury, was getting up from the floor and heading toward Blaize, his intentions plainly written on his face. Blaize, hands on hips, his expression equally readable, was waiting for him, his chest heaving. Neither man paid the slightest attention to her as she flew down the stairs. Bill lunged toward Blaize, swinging wildly. Blaize calmly ducked, led with his right hand, and then sent Bill flying with a hard left hook to his jaw. Bill stumbled backwards over Samantha's pile of huge cushions and landed on his backside, his head thumping loudly against the wall.

'You idiot, look what you've done!' she yelled at Blaize, who was rubbing his hand. She hurried to Bill's side. 'Bill, are you all right? Oh, dear, look at your poor lip.' Bill's lower lip was swollen and purplish, his eyes vague as he stared at her.

'Oh, hello, Sam. I think so,' Bill replied, trying to sit up, and then sinking back again with a groan.

Samantha took his arms and tugged at him, then looked up at Blaize, who was still silently looking at his victim, a critical frown between his dark brows.

'Help me get him to the couch,' Samantha commanded.

'I will if he's through attacking me,' Blaize replied. 'He let himself in with a key and then swung a vase at me, after calling me a few names. I pushed him away. I think you saw the rest.'

Samantha frowned at Bill, who was now struggling to his feet with her help, and then back at Blaize. Suddenly it was clear to her what must have happened. Poor Bill must have seen the Mercedes parked in front of her apartment all night and thought she'd done for Blaize what she'd never been willing to do for him, the very thought upsetting him so much that he'd come rushing over to verify his fears. A glance at the couch told her that Blaize had already been up, his bedding folded in a neat pile at one end. As upset as he was, Bill probably hadn't noticed it and had assumed that Blaize had come downstairs from her bed. Well, if he thought that she had suddenly turned into that sort of woman, he deserved what he had got.

'A fine pair you two are,' Samantha said, shaking her head, her mouth twisted in disgust. She frowned at Bill again. 'A supposedly brilliant mind, and you couldn't even take the time to find out why Blaize was here, or notice that he'd slept on the couch.' She pointed towards the pile of bedding. 'And you...' she turned her attention to Blaize '...didn't have the sense to figure out who Bill was or why he was upset. Frankly, I don't think I much care for either of you two imbeciles. My living-room is a shambles, and I can't think of a more unpleasant way to be wakened from a sound sleep. Now, while I go and get dressed, you two can straighten up the mess and start the coffee.' She started to stalk towards the stairs and then stopped and turned. Both men were staring after her, Bill still looking somewhat bewildered, and Blaize grinning broadly.

'Bill Grimes, Blaize Leighton,' she said, pointing from one to the other. 'Do take the trouble to get acquainted now.' With that, she hurried up the stairs and into her room, banging the door closed behind her. She flung off her robe and sank down on the side of her bed, buried her face in her hands, and silently laughed until the tears were running down her cheeks. It wasn't really funny that Bill had been so distressed and got his lip smashed, but the sight of the two men, obviously fighting over her, was so bizarre that she could not help laughing. Never in her wildest dreams had she imagined something like that happening to her. It was like one of Mark Westland's old movies. All it would have needed was Blaize, swinging down from her balcony, to make it complete.

Samantha quickly showered, dressed in jeans and a soft pink sweater, and hurried back downstairs, curious as to how the two men might be getting along. From the laughter she heard as she drew near the kitchen, she gathered that it was far better than she had imagined they might.

'Ah, there's Sleeping Beauty now,' Blaize said, rising from the table as Samantha poked her head around the doorframe. 'If you hadn't slept so late, our little altercation might have been avoided,' he added with a teasing smile as he pulled out a chair for Samantha to sit between him and Bill.

'Hmph. I'm darned if I'll take the blame for your Neanderthal behaviour,' she replied, taking the cup of coffee that Blaize poured for her and sitting down at the table with the two men. She raised an eyebrow at Bill, who smiled sheepishly. 'I hope you're straightened out now on why Blaize was here.'

Bill nodded. 'I don't blame him for being worried. I'd have done the same thing.' He looked at Blaize. 'Do you want to tell her what else we did because we were worried?'

'Might as well,' Blaize said. 'I told Bill about Lockwood's call, and we agreed that Mark Westland should be told, so I called him. Mark also agreed that Lockwood wasn't anyone worth endangering you for, and he's going to call him.'

Samantha scowled at them both. 'I hope you don't expect me to thank you,' she said.

'No,' said the men in unison, and then laughed so heartily that Samantha was forced to smile. Strange, she thought, that they were getting along so well now. Strange, also, that she was sure it was Blaize's doing that they were. He was one of the most insightful people she had ever known, and at the moment she felt very grateful to him for trying to make things easier for Bill. She knew they were still far from easy when, a moment later, he gave her a meaningful look.

'Blaize tells me he's taking you to Disneyland today,' he said, his voice also revealing the strain he was under.

'So he tells me,' Samantha replied, trying to sound neutral. She neither wanted Bill to think she was delighted, nor Blaize to think she was still cross about going. For some reason, the idea now sounded quite pleasant.

'Well, I'd better get going and let you two get ready,' Bill said. 'Nice to have met you.' He shook hands with Blaize.

Samantha followed him to the door, unsure of what to say. At the door, Bill turned to face her, his expression bitterly sad.

'I wish I could say I was glad you met him, because I can see he's a terrific guy,' he said, 'but I can't. I do hope you'll be happy with him, though.'

'But I'm not . . .' Samantha began, but before she could finish, Bill had slipped out the door. Feeling depressed at Bill's unhappiness, she wandered back into the kitchen, only to be greeted by a growl from Blaize.

'Why in the devil didn't you warn me about Grimes? He was ready to kill me when he first came in, and I can't say I really appreciated the way he seems to think he owns you.'

'What makes you think you do?' Samantha snapped back, surprised at the anger she saw on Blaize's face. 'You have no right at all to be jealous!'

'Does Grimes?' Blaize countered.

'No! No one does. Jealousy is a stupid, childish emotion,' Samantha said, irritated that Blaize's apparent generosity of spirit had been so shallow. 'If you're going to act like that, I won't go to Disneyland with you after all.'

Blaize smiled wryly. 'I suppose you wouldn't mind at all if you came into my house and found me in bed with another woman? Think about it now, before you answer me. Try to picture it. She has black hair and green eyes and looks like Elizabeth Taylor.'

'Oh, stop your silly games!' Samantha said, finding that the image Blaize's words created was anything but pleasant. 'You can sleep with anyone you want to, I don't care.' She looked away from Blaize's knowing smile. 'Well, I don't,' she added defiantly. There wasn't any reason why she *should* care. Not any reason at all. Did Blaize really know someone who looked like Elizabeth Taylor?

CHAPTER SIX

WHEN Samantha awoke on Monday morning, she felt as if her head were in a vice.

'I can't have drunk that much champagne,' she said, groaning as she sat up in bed, rubbing her neck. Maybe it was those crazy dreams she had all night, dreams in which she clung frantically to Blaize, screaming, as they plummeted through the Matterhorn, the wild rollercoaster of Disneyland. That ride had been the climax of a wonderful day, a return to the kind of carefree fun that Blaize had promised. He seemed to enjoy every ride, every exhibit, as much as any child, so that soon Samantha found herself immersed in his good humour, seeing the familiar sights with a fresh, enthusiastic eye. After that, loaded with souvenirs, including a giant stuffed Mickey Mouse, they had returned to Blaize's house on the beach at Malibu for a dinner of steaks and champagne—returned, because they had gone there in the morning so that Blaize could change his clothes to jeans and a sweater, and alert his cook to have dinner ready for them that evening.

The only thing that had marred the otherwise perfect day was Blaize's renewed declaration of love after he had brought Samantha home and kissed her until her knees were weak and she was clinging to him for support.

'I don't expect you to say it yet,' he had said gently when she had stared at him silently, her eyes filled with tears of confusion. 'I just wish I didn't have to go back to New York in the morning. It's going to take longer, with me going back and forth like this. Somehow I'm going to have to arrange to spend a month out here, beginning in a week or two. I'll call you every night, though.'

'No, don't,' Samantha had croaked out over the lump in her throat. 'Don't call. Don't send any flowers. Just leave me alone for a while.'

Blaize had looked at her thoughtfully for a long time. 'All right,' he had finally agreed. 'That might be a good idea. I'll see you next weekend.'

After Blaize had left, Samantha had burst into tears, hurrying upstairs to fling herself headlong on to her bed. She hadn't even bothered to undress, burying her face in her pillows and pulling the blanket up over her head.

'Good lord, that must be what's wrong with me,' Samantha said, looking down and seeing that she still had on her pink sweater. She had cried herself to sleep, something she hadn't done in years. But why had she done so? Was it because Blaize had kissed her? Because he'd said he loved her? Or because he was gone again, and next Saturday suddenly seemed very far away?

With a grimace, Samantha pushed herself out of bed and went to take a shower. What difference did it make why she had cried herself to sleep? It was a stupid thing to do. She must have been overtired or had too much champagne, or both. Now it was time to get her act together and try to remember where she and Mark Westland had left off. Oh, yes. He was going to tell her about being a spy. Maybe that had something to with the mysterious person he said he hoped to contact again through his book.

Samantha was still feeling a bit shaky when she arrived at Mark Westland's house and was ushered into his huge, rustic living-room by his dour manservant.

'I'm not sure Maxwell approves of me,' Samantha said, trying to divert Mark, who was looking at her critically.

'I'm not sure he approves of life,' Mark replied, smiling. 'How is life treating you? You look a little under the weather. Are you missing young Mr Leighton already?'

'Of course not,' Samantha replied quickly. 'I'm fine. Now, how about those spy stories you promised me last week?'

'Don't want to talk about it, hmmm?' Mark said, raising his eyebrows questioningly. 'I think maybe you should. I was rather impressed with your young man when I talked to him yesterday. I could tell by his voice that he cares for you very deeply.'

Samantha pursed her lips, avoiding the old actor's penetrating stare. 'I can't quite put my finger on what the problem is. He's a very nice person, almost too nice. Maybe that's it. I can't really believe...oh, never mind. He just gets too carried away, that's all.'

'Still deluging you with flowers? I can't believe you're tied up in knots over that. Come, Samantha, out with it. What terrible excesses has the boy committed now? Has he been too forward...or not forward enough?'

'I'd rather not discuss it,' Samantha said, swallowing hard. 'It's rather personal.'

Mark Westland leaned forward and peered closely at Samantha. 'Your eyelids are puffy. You've been crying.' With a violence that startled Samantha, he pounded his fist on the table between them. 'By God, if he's tried to harm you, I'll put every detail of my brawl with that old fool George Leighton in my book!'

'No, Mark, no!' Samantha cried. 'He hasn't done anything like that. It's just that it will sound so silly to you!'

'Try me,' Mark said, leaning back once again.

'He insists that he loves me,' Samantha said, her voice hoarse with strain, 'and that I love him, too, but I just don't know it yet. The trouble is, I don't think that can possibly be true. We've only known each other a little over a week. It's just not long enough to know something like that.' She looked beseechingly at Mark Westland. 'It makes me feel all mixed up to have him keep telling me that. Do you think he could just be saying those things to get at your book through me?'

Mark shook his head. 'I don't think there's a chance of that. Flowers and even money and seduction are one thing, but declarations of love are quite another. No one except a very unprincipled man would make them lightly, except under extreme duress, and I don't think that either description applies to Blaize Leighton, do you?' He raised his eyebrows questioningly.

'N-no,' Samantha replied. Both his actions and her intuition told her that Blaize was highly principled, and it certainly didn't sound as if his father's life contained any dark secrets that were worth compromising those principles.

'Then I think your chief problem is that he believes in love at first sight and you don't, but your emotions are at odds with your logic.'

'Maybe.' Samantha sighed heavily. 'I'm not sure what I feel any more, besides confused. Why can't he just be quiet about it for a while? If he's right, it will all work out eventually.'

'Young love is very impatient,' Mark replied.

He smiled at Samantha, but his eyes seemed to be looking right through her, seeing something or someone else. She watched his face curiously, as gradually his smile faded and look of the most tender, loving gentleness replaced it.

'Let me tell you a story,' he said at last, his eyes unnaturally bright as they returned to Samantha. 'This is very much off the record. Privileged information. Do you understand?'

'Oh, yes,' she replied quickly.

'You recall,' Mark began, 'that I told you last week of my one marriage, which ended after only a year when Susan died in childbirth. Most people have assumed that, since I never remarried, she was the one great love of my life. She was not. I loved her, but there was another young woman, just a girl when I knew her, who truly fills that description.' Mark paused and lit one of his infrequent cigarettes and then continued.

'It was ten years after Susan died, in the spring. I was in France, making one of those historical extravaganzas based loosely on something by Dumas. I was duelling among the statuary in the formal gardens of a grand estate near Paris when I caught my foot on a loose stone and went crashing backwards, damaging my pride very badly. As if that weren't enough, I heard someone behind me laughing, a very merry, girlish laugh. I got up and dusted my rear with as much dignity as I could muster, and then

turned around to give that heartless female a good
tongue-lashing. When I saw her, my heart stood still.'
He smiled in remembrance. 'She was a tiny little thing,
with short dark curls and dark eyes, roses in her
cheeks. She had on modern dress, so I knew she wasn't
a member of the cast. I wanted to run to her and ask
her her name, but I had to get on with the scene.
When I was through, she was gone. I asked around,
but no one knew who she was. I had to find her. I
wasn't a boy any more, but I was deeply, hopelessly
in love.' Mark paused again and raised his eyebrows
meaningfully at Samantha, who smiled.

'Are you sure? Did you ever find her?'

'She found me. That evening I got a note to meet
her back in that same garden. I bought a huge bouquet
of roses and went, my heart beating so hard by the
time I got there that I thought it would burst. When
we met, it was as if the earth stood still, for both of
us. We met every night for the next month, always in
a different place. Sometimes it was in the country,
sometimes in a strange little café she would know
about, sometimes in an apartment she had borrowed
from one friend or another. We talked a lot, and we
loved. Oh, how we loved!' Mark's eyes grew misty.
'She never told me any name except Anne-Marie,
never said much about her family. She spoke both
French and English equally well, so I was never sure
where her home was. I asked, I begged her to marry,
but she could not. She was much younger than me,
only nineteen, and her family had promised her hand
in marriage to an older businessman in only a few
weeks' time. Her strong sense of duty would not
permit her to go against their wishes. After a month,
she said goodbye and told me not to try to find her,

that it would bring both of us only grief. Fool that I was, I respected her wishes. If only I'd tried to find her then...' He fell silent, his eyes, closed, then roused himself with an obvious effort, his voice husky as he continued, 'A year later I got a letter from her, postmarked from Lyon. All that it said was 'We have a son. He is very like you. I still love you. Anne-Marie.' From that day to this, that is all I have ever heard. Thousands of dollars spent on detectives produced nothing at all.'

'Oh, Mark,' Samantha whispered, tears streaming unchecked down her cheeks. 'Oh, lord, how I hope your book does find her and your son for you. She's the one you meant, isn't she? The person you hoped to reach?'

Mark nodded. 'I made the publisher agree to cover the European markets. But who knows where she might be, or if she, or my son, are still alive?'

'They must be!' Samantha cried. 'They have to be!'

'Why?' Mark raised an eyebrow and gave her a crooked smile. 'You're not a romantic. You don't believe in love at first sight.'

Samantha blushed and dabbed at her eyes with a Kleenex. 'I guess sometimes it does happen,' she said softly. 'Are you going to put any message in the book for Anne-Marie?'

'I'm going to dedicate it to her,' Mark replied. 'To Anne-Marie, whom I still love.' He gave a dry little laugh. 'At the very least, it will cause a lot of speculation.'

'It will certainly do that,' Samantha agreed, imagining all of the people who would try to figure out which Hollywood star was disguised in that name, while in reality it was a simple French girl who had married some stuffy old businessman.

'If you don't mind,' Mark said suddenly, 'I don't think I feel much like working on the book today, and I don't think you do, either. Let's wait until tomorrow to get into the spy business. I'll see you to the door.'

Samantha nodded in agreement, and smiled sympathetically at the old actor as they walked slowly toward the door. Even after more than thirty-five years, thinking of his Anne-Marie was still a deeply moving experience for him.

'Maybe we can both get some extra rest tonight,' she said. 'I certainly could use it.'

'I'm more apt to sit up late, reading,' Mark said. 'It helps to keep my mind busy.' He opened the door, and then put a staying hand on Samantha's shoulder. 'If it would help to remove any doubts you still may have, I'd be happy to assure young Mr Leighton that there will be no mention of his father in my book.'

'I-I don't think that's necessary,' Samantha replied. 'I guess I was overly suspicious.' After hearing Mark's story, she felt quite sure that Blaize meant it when he said he loved her. Apparently, some people did fall in love in a matter of minutes. Whether anything like that could happen to her, she still had her doubts. Blaize might send her emotions into a tailspin, but surely that wasn't all there was to love.

While she drove to her apartment, thoughts kept chasing themselves through Samantha's mind like squirrels around a tree trunk. Could she be in love with Blaize? Surely she'd know it if she were. But how? There were enough bells ringing and sparks flying. What did she expect? A little sign that popped up in front of her eyes, saying 'This is it, Samantha.

This is the real thing.'? No, of course not. That was ridiculous. Maybe what she had expected was fewer sparks. Something more calm and collected, that made her feel warm and secure, not nervous and jittery. Something in between the intellectual companionship she had with Bill and the emotional madhouse she felt when Blaize was near.

'Maybe I don't know what I want,' she muttered to herself, wishing that Mark had not called off their session for the day. Going home to an apartment empty of flowers, with no telephone call to look forward to, held no appeal at all. She did not want to analyse why that might be. She needed to find something to distract her, but she was too over-wrought to read or do research. Suddenly a sign caught her eye: 'Video Rentals - World's Largest Selection.' The perfect thing! She would get some of Mark Westland's old movies to watch on her VCR! A short time later, clutching a stack of videotapes, she was on her way again, smiling to herself over the astonishment of the young clerk who had remarked on the sudden interest in Mark Westland movies.

'We've had to order more ever since it got out that he's writing his memoirs. Is that why you want these?'

'Oh, no, I've always been a fan of his,' Samantha had told him soberly. 'They don't make romantic heroes like him any more. I just wish you had the first movie he made, when he sang and danced. *Nights of Romance*, I think it was called.'

'It's not in the book,' the young man had said, checking his listings, 'but I expect they'll come out with it now. Leave your name and phone number, and I'll call you when they do.'

By midnight, Samantha was bleary-eyed from watching Mark Westland swashbuckle his way through heart-stopping adventures and romance his way into the hearts of innumerable gorgeous damsels. There was no doubt that he had been even more handsome in action than in the still photographs she'd seen, his black wavy hair shoulderlength in his pirate roles, his narrow black moustache accenting the gleaming white of his devilish smile. And, tame though the love scenes were in movies of that period, it was easy to imagine that far more went on than was shown on the screen. The gleam in Mark's charismatic blue eyes was too seductive to deny. If Mark were thirty years younger, Blaize Leighton would have some real competition. As it was, Samantha found it very easy to imagine Blaize in one of Mark's roles. There was something about the way they moved and smiled that was very similar. And then there was that cleft in their chins...

'I wonder if Blaize ever had fencing lessons?' Samantha mused aloud. Put him in a period costume and hand him a foil and he would be spectacular. Not that he wasn't quite special in modern dress. He had such nice broad shoulders to lean on...

'I am not going to think about him this week!' Samantha announced loudly, banging her fist down on the top of her television set and sending her dogs into a frenzy of barking at the loud noise. 'Sorry guys,' she said to the excited pair. 'False alarm. Just talking to myself. Why don't you two entertain me so I won't do that any more? That would keep me from thinking about Mr Leighton, too. Then, when I see him again, I might be able to tell more about how I really feel. What do you think?' She smiled wryly at the two pairs of bright eyes watching her expectantly, the two tails wagging hopefully. 'You two don't give a darn about my problems. All you want is a puppy biscuit. All right, come on. Then it's time for bed.'

'You can't blame me for hoping two days without flowers meant you and Leighton had broken up,' Bill Grimes said the next morning when, having received a negative response to his question, he flopped down on Samantha's sofa, looking glum.

'You can't break up something that isn't together,' Samantha snapped crossly. 'Why do you persist in creating something out of nothing?'

'Leighton doesn't think it's nothing,' Bill replied. 'He looks at you like Slim looking at a fresh T-bone steak.'

'That's his problem,' Samantha retorted, frowning. She had been doing fairly well, avoiding thinking about Blaize, until Bill had shown up. Fairly well. At least once an hour, thoughts of Blaize intruded, bringing whatever project she was working on to a screeching halt. At this rate, it was going to seem like four years until Saturday, not four days. Oh, why had she told him not to call or send any flowers? Last night she had almost called his home, but a kind of foreboding stayed her hand at the last moment, as if breaking her self-imposed silence would also break the magic spell, and Blaize and all of the roses would turn out to have been only a dream. She had even, foolishly, rushed to look at her yard, half expecting it to be the drab little place it once was.

'Can't we talk about something else?' she said suddenly, to break her strange chain of thoughts. 'How is your work going? How is Monica?'

'OK,' Bill replied. 'I'm taking her to Disneyland on Saturday. Thought I'd see if the magic kingdom would work for me.'

'It won't if you look so sour,' Samantha said, eyeing Bill critically. 'Why don't you lighten up a bit? Quit trying to carry the weight of the world around with you all the time. It can manage without you for a while.'

'Aha!' Bill sat forward and pointed a finger at Samantha. 'Now I know I was right. Leighton's got you right where he wants you, hasn't he?'

'I don't know what you're talking about,' Samantha replied, fidgeting uncomfortably in the face of Bill's accusing stare. What if she had said something that sounded more like Blaize Leighton than the usual Samantha Bennet? There was nothing wrong with getting a little change in viewpoint.

'Come on, Sam, you're not that dense,' Bill said, wagging his finger at her again. 'You've been playing female Atlas for years, and now all of a sudden you've got a whole new perspective. If that doesn't mean you're in love with Blaize Leighton, I don't know what would.'

'It doesn't mean any such thing,' Samantha denied hotly. 'I was only trying to help you charm Monica. You can take my advice or leave it. Now, if you don't mind, I have to get to work.'

'I'll take it,' Bill said, grinning as he headed for the door. 'After all, it worked for Leighton.'

'You might try some decent clothes, too,' Samantha called after his disappearing form. When the door had closed behind him, she sighed and shook her head. Bill might not be elegant and charming, but he was very astute. Maybe he was right. Maybe she *was* in love with Blaize. There must be some reason she couldn't get him out of her mind. She'd have to try harder. There were a lot of things she needed to think about, including Mark Westland's book. His spy adventures ought to be interesting enough to keep her from going berserk before Blaize returned.

By Thursday night, Samantha was forced to admit that there was probably nothing fascinating enough to keep her mind off of Blaize for more than a few hours at a time. She would be working hard at the book, think she was concentrating, and suddenly find herself staring into space, picturing how Blaize had looked when he lay on her sofa, beckoning to her, or how he had looked when he climbed out of the trench, or how that scar must look. If this was love, she mused wryly, it was the most uncomfortable disease she had ever experienced. Even with a bad case of the 'flu, she could still keep her mind on her work.

When the same thing happened for the fourth time in one hour on Friday evening, she turned off her computer and gave up the struggle. It was only seven o'clock, but she might as well take a shower and then sit and stare at the television and dream of Blaize. Maybe he'd arranged to take over her mind in preparation for his return. He was capable of other kinds of magic.

She had just stepped out of the shower when her doorbell rang and Slim and Poco went into an unusually high-pitched barking routine.

'Must be someone they know,' Samantha muttered, wrapping a towel around her wet hair and slipping into her terry robe and slippers. She could hear the sound of their feet, pawing at the door. She hurried downstairs, paused to make her robe and towel secure, and then said loudly, 'Who is it?'

'Florist's delivery,' said an oddly scratchy voice. 'Got some roses for a Miss Samantha Bennet.'

'Just set them by the door,' Samantha said. 'I'll get them in a few minutes.'

'The hell you will!' boomed a loud, familiar deep voice. 'Let me in, woman!'

'Blaize!' Samantha cried, flinging the door wide.

It was only a matter of seconds before Blaize had stepped inside, closed the door behind him, and enveloped Samantha in his arms, but she already had the answer she had been seeking. At the very sight of his warm smile, the happiness in his dark eyes, a great joy had set her heart singing. When Blaize had opened his arms, she had gone to him willingly, her own arms holding him close, her lips meeting his eagerly.

'What are you doing here now?' she managed to gasp when he drew back his head to look at her.

'I'll explain later,' he replied, his mouth finding hers again in a kiss that left her soaring giddily. His hands found their way inside her robe, which had come partly open, and he groaned. 'Oh, lord,' and bent to sweep her into his arms.

Her robe fell open, the towel fell from her damp hair, but Samantha did not care as Blaize carried her to the sofa and sat down with her on his lap, his hands caressing her bare skin until she felt on fire with love and longing. 'God, how I want you,' he whispered next to her ear. 'I love you so very much, my darling.'

'I love you, too,' Samantha whispered back, feeling a strange thrill go through her at actually saying those words. She smiled tremulously as Blaize raised his head and gazed into her eyes, a look of wonder on his face.

'Say that again,' he said softly.

'I love you,' she replied shyly.

'Oh, thank God,' Blaize said, holding her close again, his hands stroking her eagerly. 'That makes it so much easier.'

'Easier?' Samantha asked, puzzled. 'What do you mean?'

Blaize drew his head back and smiled ruefully. 'I mean it makes it a little easier to tell you I can only stay a few minutes and then I have to leave again. My poor mother's made herself ill, worrying over that book of Mark Westland's. Her health is so frail that I shouldn't have left her right now, but I thought I'd take a chance and come to see you, if only for a few moments, and try to persuade you to ask Mark to leave whatever it is that's worrying my mother so much out of his book. I was so afraid that, if you were still denying you cared for me, you would pull back into your shell again, and then I'd have to start all over.' He brushed Samantha's lips with his own and then frowned. 'What's wrong, love?'

'N-nothing,' Samantha replied. Nothing, except that inside, where all of the lovely, warm, glowing feelings had been only moments ago, there was now nothing but a cold, terrible ache. All she wanted now was for Blaize Leighton to go away and never come back. She had been right from the start, and had been completely, terribly betrayed, not only by Blaize, but by her own emotions. Never, ever again would she let them take over her life. Not even now, when she felt a murderous rage beginning to replace her anguish.

She would not give Blaize Leighton the satisfaction of seeing her that way. She would be perfectly calm.

'Something is,' Blaize said, making a small *moue* and frowning. 'Is it that I have to leave so soon?'

Samantha nodded, wishing that Blaize would take his hands away so that she could escape their fiery touch. 'Please,' she said hoarsely, letting a few little tears escape from her eyes, 'don't do that now. I can't bear it.'

With a regretful smile, Blaize removed his hands and tucked Samantha's robe around her again. 'Neither can I,' he said, 'but when I come back we'll have a night to remember, I promise. Meantime, you will talk to Mark?'

'Yes,' Samantha agreed, blinking rapidly to prevent the tears from falling even faster. She tried to hold herself rigid as Blaize pulled her close again and kissed her, but could not, her body reacting with a surge of longing in spite of everything she could do.

Blaize released her slowly, then carefully stood up, still holding her in his arms.

'I wish I could take you with me,' he said, 'but Mother's in no condition to meet you right now. I don't know how soon I'll be back, but I'll call. You can let me know what Mark says.' He set Samantha on her feet, and caressed her hair back from her forehead. 'I think I like you best like this, all tousled and sweet,' he said, smiling his slanted smile, his eyes so deliciously warm that Samantha felt almost physically ill at the knowledge of how little that seductive look meant. He flung his arms around Samantha and held her close. 'God, how I wish I didn't have to go,' he said, his voice harsh and agonised-sounding.

Leaning against him, listening to the heavy, hard pounding of his heart, Samantha could only cling to him, scarcely able to breathe. At his words, all she could think was, And how I wish you hadn't come at all.

CHAPTER SEVEN

SAMANTHA was completely numb. After Blaize left, she sank down on her couch and sat, staring straight ahead, her mind a blank. How long she sat that way, she had no idea. Only Poco, flinging herself on to Samantha's lap and licking her face, finally awakened her from her trance. The world suddenly snapped back into focus.

'I'm here, baby, I'm here,' Samantha said, hugging the tiny dog. 'It's all right, you guys, I'm not dead.' She patted Slim, who had put his paw on her knee. 'It's just you two and me again,' she said, sighing heavily. She stood up, her body feeling detached, as if it didn't really belong to her. Why didn't she feel anything? After the first, terrible anguish, everything had stopped. Her head seemed perfectly clear now. Exceptionally clear. She could remember exactly what Blaize had said, but it didn't seem to mean anything especially disturbing. She did feel cold, probably because her hair was still damp. She must get it dry and put on some clothes, before she caught a cold. Then she must decide what to do. Blaize Leighton would call and call until he got the answer he wanted. He would tell her he loved her and send more flowers until then, no doubt. It would be interesting to find out how he planned to break it off when the issue of Mark Westland's book was over.

Floating along like an automaton, Samantha went up the stairs. Pausing at the doorway to her study, she looked at her computer and shook her head. All of that effort on Blaize's part because of that one silly little episode of his father's. His mother was certainly strange, blowing up something like that out of all proportion. Of course, she thought wryly, she couldn't really fault Blaize's devotion to his mother, if he really didn't know what it was his mother was worried about. But that might not be true, either.

Her eyes fell on the telephone next to her desk. It might ring as soon as Blaize got back to New York. He would keep the pressure on, she was sure. She'd better unplug her phones until she had decided what to say and do. She walked over and unplugged it, then went into her bedroom and unplugged the one by her bed. Next she dried her hair, admiring her own calm face with a certain haughty detachment. Whatever was all that romatic nonsense about broken hearts? She certainly didn't have one. It was over. So what? It was more of a relief than anything.

Dressed and back downstairs, Samantha unplugged her one remaining phone, let her dogs out, then poured herself a cup of coffee and sat down at her kitchen table. It was time to make some decisions about what to do. What were her choices? She picked up her notepad, set it before her and wrote down the number one. After it, she wrote, 'Tell Blaize tomorrow that I went to see Mark and he agreed to leave the story out.' It wouldn't be true, of course. Mark was gone this weekend. But he had said he'd assure Blaize the story wouldn't be in, and it would get things over with.

Samantha drummed her fingertips on the tabletop. No, she wouldn't do that. She'd as soon Blaize and his mother suffered a while longer. They deserved it.

Number two, she wrote, 'Tell Blaize that Mark refuses to leave the story out.' It would be fascinating to see what might happen then. Would they offer Mark or her some money? No, probably not. That was blackmail. But they might try something more unpleasant. Threats of some kind. Poor Mark didn't deserve that.

Number three. Samantha frowned. What else could she do? Oh, yes. 'Tell Blaize I don't love him, won't talk to him ever again, and refuse to talk to Mark.' At least the first part was true. But that would really throw the whole problem into Mark's lap. No, that wasn't fair. Drat! There must be something she could do to give Blaize Leighton the come-uppance he deserved. She got up and let her dogs back in, then paced back and forth from her front door to the back, her two pets following, curious at their mistress's strange behaviour.

It was going to be difficult to get even, Samantha reasoned, given that Blaize had just been pretending all along. However, he probably did have his ego involved, having been, he thought, so successful. What if she strung him along for a few more days, then followed number one? Then, when Blaize tried to wriggle out of their romance, she would laugh in his face and tell him what a fool he'd been to think he'd actually convinced her of his love. He was the one who had been fooled. If she could stay as cool as she was now, she should be able to give him quite a nasty jolt. Well, why shouldn't she stay cool? She felt absolutely nothing except contempt for Blaize Leighton. The slate had been wiped clean.

'Shall we watch the news?' Samantha said to her still following dogs. She went to her television, stopped, and stared. How had that box got there, on top of her TV? She hadn't seen Blaize put it there. More roses, no doubt. A quick glance inside confirmed the fact. Should she just toss them in the bin? No, why not take them to Shady Oaks tomorrow, where they would be appreciated?

Quickly, Samantha put the roses in water, throwing out the box and the accompanying card without even looking at it. Then she returned to her living-room, turned on her television, and called Slim and Poco to join her on her sofa.

'This is more like it,' she said, smiling in satisfaction as she stretched out with Poco curled up on her stomach and Slim beside her. No more annoying Blaize Leighton to worry about. She could live her own life the way she wanted to again. As the news reports droned on, she closed her eyes. The next thing she heard was the ringing of her doorbell and the barking of her dogs.

'Good heavens, it's morning!' Samantha said, rubbing her eyes. She had slept as if she'd been drugged. With an effort, she pushed herself from the clutches of her soft sofa and got to her feet, still feeling woozy. What time was it? God lord, her watch said ten o'clock!

'More roses, Miss Bennet,' said the cheerful delivery man, handing her another long, white box.

'Thanks,' Samantha said weakly, giving him a wan smile and taking the box. She closed the door and stared at the box. Something about the very idea of roses made her feel slightly sick. She hurried into her kitchen, took the card from the box and threw it away, then closed the box hurriedly. No need to put these in water. She'd be leaving for Shady Oaks soon. Thank goodness Bill was off with Monica this morning. She didn't think she could cope with any of his remarks today. Poor Bill! She'd have to set him straight on how things were now. He'd be glad she'd come to her senses.

A short time later, Samantha was on her way to the Shady Oaks Rest Home, her stomach still feeling queasy. The smell of those roses didn't help any, she thought grimly. At least she'd be rid of them soon.

At the home, Samantha was deluged with questions about Blaize Leighton. Where was he today? When was he coming back? She tried to answer calmly, but found it difficult. There was something about those eager smiles that reminded her how she must have looked and felt about Blaize. Poor things. She left much sooner than usual, feeling depressed. She'd be better off working on Mark's book.

Back at her apartment, Samantha set doggedly to work, and kept at it all day, in spite of an increasing uneasiness, the kind of sensation she sometimes had when she felt that someone was watching her. She half expected to turn around and find Blaize standing in her doorway, and did turn her head several times, then cursed herself for being a fool. He wasn't here. She didn't want him here! Ever!

She went to bed, but found she couldn't sleep; strange, shadowy images of Blaize appeared every time she closed her eyes. Soon they began appearing in the darkness of her room even with her eyes open. With a muffled curse, she got up, turned on the lights, then went downstairs, turned on all the lights, and closed her curtains. No one was going to haunt her, not even someone with the diabolical powers of Blaize Leighton. She'd watch television all night if she had to. Which was exactly what she had to do, finally falling asleep from sheer exhaustion just as the sun came up. For a second time, it was her doorbell that awakened her. Groggily, she struggled to the door, dreading the thought of the florist's delivery man and his cheery smile.

'What the hell is going on?' Bill asked as soon as she opened her door.

'Going on? Nothing,' Samantha replied, staring at him dazedly. 'Why?'

'I just got a call from Blaize Leighton. He's been trying to call you for twenty-four hours and gets no answer. Is your phone out of order?'

Samantha shook her head. 'No. I've unplugged them. Come on in and have some coffee and I'll tell you all about it.'

Over coffee, Samantha told Bill of Blaize's visit and her subsequent decision about how to handle the problem.

'You'll never be able to do it,' Bill said, shaking his head sadly. 'You may think you're over him, but you're not. You look like death warmed up. How much did you sleep last night?'

'Not much, but I had a touch of the 'flu,' Samantha replied, frowning. 'I *am* over him, if there was anything to be over.' Having Bill there to spar with was renewing her determination. In fact, having Bill there was very nice. Much better than having Blaize Leighton there, getting her upset. If she had any sense, she'd marry Bill, if he was still available. 'How was your date with Monica yesterday?' she asked.

'OK,' Bill said with a shrug. 'Nothing spectacular. Why?'

'I was just thinking what a much better couple you and I make than Blaize and I would. In fact, I was thinking of proposing to you.'

'Oh, Samantha!' Bill shook his head and rubbed his eyes. 'I've prayed for that so long, but right now isn't the time. I have no desire to catch you on the rebound and have you regret it later. If you still want to propose to me in six months, I'll listen. Meanwhile, why don't you plug your phones back in and then go back to bed? I'll call Leighton back and tell him you've got the 'flu and don't want to be disturbed until later. OK?'

'All right,' Samantha agreed with a sigh. 'You do think I'm doing the right thing, don't you?'

'I guess so,' Bill replied, frowning thoughtfully. 'Somehow, though, it doesn't all quite fit. I would have sworn that Leighton was crazy about you. He's either one hell of an actor, or else there's something else going on.'

'What kind of something else?' Samantha asked, puzzled. Bill's response hadn't been quite what she expected, either to her story of Blaize's treachery or her proposal. He was always analytical about things, but she'd thought he'd be more upset about what Blaize had done, and happier about her renewed interest in him.

'Well,' Bill said, scratching his neck and chewing his lip simultaneously, 'it seems to me it's possible that there's a lot more that Westland knows than he's letting on. Not that it's anything he plans to put in his book, but whatever it is might be enough to make Mrs Leighton worry herself sick. Why don't you push the old guy a bit and see?'

'I don't think ... well, I suppose it's worth a try,' Samantha replied reluctantly.

'Good. Now scoot back to bed. You look awful,' Bill said, grinning as Samantha made a face at him. 'That doesn't help,' he added. 'Even I wouldn't marry that face.'

'Forget I asked,' Samantha retorted. 'I've changed my mind.'

Back in bed, Samantha lay staring at her ceiling, turning over Bill's statements in her mind. What if he was right? He had implied that Blaize might really love her. Could that be possible? A knot formed in her stomach and a lump in her throat. No, she told herself, no! Bill hadn't been here; he hadn't heard what Blaize had said. And yes, Blaize probably was a good actor. He'd said that was what he'd really wanted to be. Instead of sleeping, she'd better get up and be ready when Blaize called. She wanted her mind to be functioning at top speed when he did.

It was late afternoon when the call finally came. In spite of hours of rehearsing how she would calmly pick up the phone, Samantha found her hand trembling and her heart thumping erratically when she did.

'Hello?' she croaked, her voice suddenly failing her.

'Samantha, my darling little love. How are you feeling? I've been so worried about you, I haven't been able to do a damn thing all day.'

That deep, soft voice sounded so genuinely anxious that Samantha felt a huge lump form in her already tight throat. Don't cry, you idiot! she told herself severely. He's acting!

'I'm feeling much better,' she lied. 'Just one of those twenty-four-hour bugs, I think. Nothing to worry about. H-how are you?' She had gone over and over the kind of things she should say, so that she would sound like the woman who had declared her love to Blaize on Friday night.

'Much better now, too. I'll have to get you an answering machine so that next time you don't want to answer your phone you don't scare me to death. It's a terrible affliction, being so much in love with someone that you'd die if anything happened to them. As it is, I hate being so far away when you need me. Can you pretend I'm there, and have my arms around you? That's where I wish I was.'

Samantha had known Blaize would say something like that, but it had done little good to think about it beforehand. Something in the gentle way he said it, the warmth that seemed to fly effortlessly across three thousand miles and straight into her heart, undid her shaky control. Tears began rolling down her cheeks, and when she tried to quell them she let out a sob instead.

'Oh, Samantha, you poor, lonesome angel! Don't cry, love. I'll be there as soon as the doctor says my mother's out of danger.' Blaize's voice sounded harsh with anguish.

Which would be as soon as she talked to Mark, Samantha thought bitterly, the ache in her heart making her cry even harder. 'Wh-what's wrong with your mother?' she managed to gasp out, trying to stop her tears with a dam of Kleenex.

'She had heart bypass surgery last summer, and the stress seems to have caused an arrhythmia that they're trying to get under control,' Blaize explained. 'They're trying to do it with medication, but if that doesn't work she'll have to have a pacemaker.'

'Oh, dear,' Samantha said, feeling suddenly guilty at her plan to make the woman suffer longer. She wanted to say she'd ask Mark the first thing in the morning, but bit her tongue. She was going to have to get herself under better control before she asked Mark anything. If he suspected something was amiss, he might dig in his heels and refuse to do anything helpful. Instead she said, 'I'll speak to Mark as soon as I can, but I have to bring it up tactfully. I hope you understand.'

'Of course I do,' Blaize replied. 'I trust your instincts completely.'

'My instincts aren't all that good,' Samantha said sadly. Here she was, trying desperately to remember that Blaize Leighton wasn't to be trusted, while at the same time she felt herself wishing he was really here to hold her in his arms. Whatever had happened to that wonderful, calm detachment she had felt after he had left on Friday night? She was going to have to try to get it back before she faced Mark Westland.

She hoped she had done so by the next afternoon, but one glance from Mark's penetrating blue eyes told her that she was still on shaky ground. If she told him about Blaize's request, she would surely burst into tears, and the game would be up. Instead, she tried to listen attentively to Mark's stories of some of his famous rows with various directors.

'I'll work it in somehow tomorrow,' she told Blaize that night. 'There's no point in putting it off, if it will help your mother.' And help Samantha Bennet, too, she thought wryly. Many more nights of listening to Blaize's declarations of love and longing would give her a heart condition, too. She did love him, after all, in spite of everything. She admitted it now. The next thing was to put an end to these nightly torture sessions and start to get over him.

The next afternoon, with that thought firmly in mind, Samantha brought up Blaize's request to Mark Westland. She also followed Bill's advice.

'Are you sure you don't know something else about George Leighton?' she asked. 'Something you may have forgotten before? Somehow, that little street brawl doesn't seem scandalous enough to send someone to the hospital.

Mark shook his head. 'No, I really don't know anything else, Samantha,' he replied. 'And I certainly don't object to your assuring Blaize Leighton that we'll leave out all references to his father. Do you suppose his mother is a little unbalanced?'

'I've wondered about that,' Samantha replied. 'My only other hypothesis is that she had good reason to suspect her husband told you something very incriminating that he either didn't tell you or that you've forgotten. Maybe he even told her that he did, for some reason.'

'I can't imagine stodgy old George having been up to anything exciting,' Mark said, frowning. 'I wish I could remember what he was babbling about before he took that swing at me, but his speech was so slurred and it's been so long...'

'Could he have said something about his wife?' Samantha asked. 'That might make her more upset than something about himself. Blaize told me she was much more lively and outgoing than his father. I gathered they didn't get along too well.'

'Could be.' Mark smiled wryly. 'Maybe, given my reputation, he took that swing at me on behalf of all men whose wives have gone astray. I never could convince the press that I didn't fool around with married women.'

'After looking at some of your movies, I can see why,' Samantha teased. 'That gleam in your eyes was positively lethal.'

'Hmph,' Mark said, looking embarrassed. 'Be that as it may, why don't you assure young Leighton that there will be no mention of his family at all, on the off chance that it's something about herself that has the poor lady in such a stew?'

'I'll do that,' Samantha agreed. 'Now, what shall we talk about today? More fights with directors?' She turned on her tape recorder as Mark chuckled and began, 'There was one more...'

On her way home, Samantha stopped at the video rental shop again to return the tapes she had rented and see if some more were available.

'I'm glad you came in, Miss Bennet,' the assistant said. 'I tried to call you this afternoon. We have *Nights of Romance* now.'

'Wonderful,' Samantha said. It would be something to distract her while she waited for Blaize's call. He had said he might be late tonight. Something about a meeting. Watching Mark's first movie would keep her from wondering what kind of a meeting it was. She had found herself speculating about that black-haired woman who looked like Elizabeth Taylor.

As soon as Samantha had finished her dinner, she popped the tape of *Nights of Romance* into her VCR and sat down to watch. No sooner had she pressed the remote button than her telephone rang.

'Drat,' she said, turning it off again and going to her kitchen phone. It was too early to be Blaize calling, but the sound of the ring had set her stomach to churning. 'Hello,' she said sharply.

'You sound grouchy enough,' said Bill's voice. 'Did your little piece of information for Leighton work that fast, or haven't you told him yet?'

'Not yet. Tonight,' Samantha replied. 'I'm all tied in knots. Want to come over? I've got Mark Westland's first movie here on the VCR. It's the song and dance one.'

'Be right there,' Bill replied.

With a sigh of relief, Samantha took a beer from her refrigerator for Bill and went to unlock her front door. It would help to have Bill here to talk to. She already had a sense of foreboding hanging over her like a black cloud.

'Let the show begin,' Bill said, as soon as he had flopped down on the sofa and popped the top of his beer can. 'This ought to be something. Black and white, I suppose?'

'Oh, yes. And scratchy music and titles that look like some kid cut them out of shiny paper.' She started the tape, then tucked her feet under her and leaned back.

The first part of the movie involved the heroine, a blonde *ingénue* from a small town who aspired to the bright lights of Broadway. Her great hope was to dance in some famous revue. She struggled to New York, went to the theatre to audition. There, waiting to try out, were dozens of young men and women. One unfortunate maiden was sent away in tears. One young man got a similar reception.

'I'll bet our hero is up next,' Bill said drily. 'That's always the way...' Suddenly he leaned forward. 'My God!' he cried. 'It's him!' He looked over at Samantha, who had gone pale as a ghost. 'What the hell...good lord, Sam, are you all right?'

Samantha shook her head back and forth, her heart pounding so hard it made her shake.

'No!' she cried. 'No! It can't be! But it is!'

'Here, give me that,' Bill said, taking the remote control from Samantha's trembling hand. He backed the tape up and froze a frame on a close-up of Mark Westland's face. 'That,' he said very positively, 'is Blaize Leighton's twin.'

'No, it isn't,' Samantha said in a hushed voice. 'That is Blaize Leighton's father.' Mark Westland, very young, with no moustache, and hair that was not long and black but short, lighter coloured and curly, was so much like Blaize Leighton that they could have been at least fraternal twins.

'What the hell are you talking about?' Bill demanded.

'That might explain everything,' Samantha said, talking as if to herself. 'If Mrs Leighton is really Anne-Marie, and her husband knew about her and Mark Westland, and...'

'Samantha!' Bill roared. 'Back up that tape in your head and start it over.'

Samantha looked at Bill. 'I...I can't,' she said. 'I promised Mark. But...' Desperately, she tried to think things through, to quickly make sense of what seemed to be true. It was still so scrambled, so strange. If she could tell Bill, he might be some help. 'Can you keep a very big secret?' she asked.

'You know damn well I can,' Bill replied.

'All right.' Her hands knotted together, Samantha repeated Mark's story of Anne-Marie almost word for word, then Mark's description of his fight with George

Leighton. 'If George Leighton knew, it would certainly explain his taking a swing at Mark,' she said. 'But Mark doesn't know a thing about Mrs Leighton. Why should she be so worried?'

'It's obvious,' Bill replied. 'She thinks Mark does know, and that George told him. Maybe George told her he did, but he was so drunk that he really didn't. Or he told her he did just so the poor woman would think Mark Westland is a real bastard.'

'What do you mean?' Samantha asked, puzzled.

'Simple. If Mark knew all this time and never contacted her, she'd think he never did love her after all, and doesn't give a damn about his son. Given that, he'd be apt to tell all in his book, like some dirty little story.'

'That makes sense,' Samantha said. 'But...do you suppose that Blaize really has no idea? I mean, why wouldn't his mother have told him by now? His father's dead.'

'How do you tell someone that his father isn't his father after all, especially when he was named after him?' Bill asked drily. 'That sort of thing isn't done in the Leightons' social circle. In fact, they probably made Blaize a 'Junior' just to remove any suspicion, since he was undoubtedly born less than nine months after the wedding. No, I doubt Blaize has any idea. Even if he's seen some old Westland movies, he probably only thought the resemblance was a coincidence.'

'It wasn't nearly so striking in the later movies,' Samantha said. 'Mark either wore a black wig or they dyed his hair and straightened it a bit. He always had a moustache, too, and sometimes a beard, and in those period costumes he wore... I thought it was just co-incidence myself. I suppose it still could be.'

'Not likely,' Bill said. 'Not likely at all.'

'No, I guess not,' Samantha said weakly. But what a strange conspiracy of events had brought everything together. In her mind's eye, images of Mark, Blaize, and Anne-Marie as Mark had described her skittered about like kaleidoscopic fragments of a puzzle. They were so close together now, and yet still so far apart. Only she held the key to putting the puzzle together. But could she? Should she? A huge lump formed in her throat.

'Oh, Bill,' she said hoarsely, 'what on earth shall I do?'

CHAPTER EIGHT

'THINK long and hard before you do anything,' Bill advised soberly. 'Wait and see what Blaize does after you've told him Mark won't mention the Leightons. Maybe the best thing will be to do nothing at all. Switching fathers after over thirty years would be a pretty big shock. It's not an item you hurl at someone you're not getting along with.'

'Oh, no,' Samantha agreed quickly. 'I don't know how I'd begin to tell either Blaize or Mark.'

'You'll find a way when the time is right,' Bill said, squeezing her hand comfortingly. 'Now, shall we watch the rest of the movie?'

Samantha nodded and sighed. 'Might as well.' She sat transfixed, watching the man who could be Blaize, feeling as if it were Blaize she was watching. She loved it when he smiled and sang, and felt as if she were in his arms when he kissed the heroine. She wanted to fling her arms around him and comfort him when the fickle woman seemed about to choose another, wealthier man. Her eyes grew misty when at last true love conquered all.

'Either you're a real sucker for a romance, or else you're so much in love with Blaize Leighton that you're living vicariously,' Bill commented when the movie ended.

'Both,' Samantha admitted sadly. 'I'm a mess.'

'Not really,' Bill said. 'Just human.'

The telephone rang and Samantha started, looking towards the sound apprehensively.

'That's probably Blaize now.'

'Then answer it. I'll let myself out,' Bill said. 'See you later.'

Samantha nodded, gave Bill a weak smile, and hurried towards her phone. This was going to have been a difficult enough call, and now it was even worse. She'd have to be very careful what she said. She must give no clue that anything was different, when, in fact, everything was. She cleared her throat and reached for the phone.

'Hello,' she said, her voice cracking in spite of her best efforts to sound bright and cheerful.

'Hello, angel. How's my love? You sound as if you're still a little choked up.'

At the sound of that deep, warm voice, Samantha's knees turned to jelly and she grabbed for a chair and sat down quickly.

'I'm fine,' she replied. 'It's the blasted smog, I think. There was one of those alerts today for people with respiratory problems. Maybe I'm one of them.'

'I hope not,' Blaize said, sounding concerned. 'Has it bothered you before?'

'No, of course not,' Samantha said, trying to get herself under better control. 'I've lived here all my life, and I'm tough as nails. How are things in New York?'

'Lousy. Cold and drizzly. Typical March weather in the Big Apple. It's never bothered me before, either, but right now I miss you so much it's like a huge, grey blanket that takes the joy out of everything. I'd like to chuck it all and get on the first plane to come and see you.'

'Oh, Blaize,' Samantha said hoarsely. How she wished she could really believe he meant that! 'I wish you could do that,' she said. 'I got the roses. They always make me think of you.'

'What about the cards?' Blaize asked.

Samantha felt a twinge of guilt. Why hadn't she at least looked at them? Knowing Blaize, he had probably thought of new and imaginative ways to declare his love. 'I—I was overwhelmed,' she said. 'I've got them under my pillow.'

Blaize chuckled. 'I thought you might be. I'm glad you didn't throw them out. At least I've made that much progress.'

At that comment, Samantha frowned. Why would she have thrown them out? She'd already told him she loved him. Maybe he didn't quite believe it yet. Perhaps she should tell him again. If he really loved her, he would be glad to hear it. If he didn't it might help to make him feel guilty for deceiving her.

'You've made more progress than that,' she said. 'You know that I love you. I can't stand having you so far away. But you should be able to come back soon. I talked to Mark today about . . . you know.'

'Really?' Blaize's voice took on a new, alert dimension. 'What did he say?'

'He said to tell you not to worry. Your mother, too. There won't be any mention of the Leightons in his book.' Samantha held her breath, waiting to try and get some clue about Blaize's reaction from his reply.

'That's wonderful news,' Blaize said. 'Samantha, I don't know how to thank you. I know you didn't really want to have to ask that favour from Mark, and if it hadn't been for mother's illness, I would never have asked you to.'

Samantha's heart gave a hopeful little skip. Blaize sounded perfectly sincere. Had she been wrong? Oh, if only she had!

'I didn't mind,' she said. 'I just hope your mother feels better very soon. I don't think I'll even notice if the smog lifts until you're here again.'

'What a sweet thing to say,' Blaize said, his voice like velvet again. 'Perhaps the best thing for me to do now is to say goodnight and then call Mother with the good news. The sooner she recovers, the sooner we can be together again.'

'Yes,' Samantha agreed. 'I think you're right.'

'Goodnight, then, my love. How about a long-distance kiss? Close your eyes. I'm putting my arms around you now. There, that's right. Now, don't move.'

Samantha smiled to herself, shivering dreamily as she imagined Blaize's arms around her, her eyes closed and her lips puckered slightly. She heard a little kissing sound and then made one of her own.

'Lovely,' Blaize breathed softly. 'I'll call you tomorrow. Dream of me tonight, will you?'

'Of course. I always do,' Samantha replied, her heart singing as she hung up the phone, but her fingers still crossed so hard her knuckles hurt. So far, at least, it didn't sound as if Blaize were trying to let her down from her romantic heights. She could have been wrong. Concern for his mother might have been Blaize's only motive, after all. But even that renewed hope did not remove her other terrible problem. What to do with her secret?

Seeing Mark the next day only compounded Samantha's confusion. Before they started taping, Mark remarked casually how amazing it was that old

George Leighton had produced a son who was so warm and loving, both towards Samantha and towards his mother. Almost undone, Samantha could only croak out, 'It certainly is!' and hope that she hadn't looked too startled by Mark's words. She longed to be able to tell him that his quest was finally over, but knew that she must not. First of all, she must be absolutely sure that she was right, that Blaize was indeed Mark's long-lost son. Even then, she would probably not begin by telling Mark.

For hours the previous night she had pondered the problem of how, when, and whether to begin to put the pieces of the puzzle together. If Blaize truly loved her, she had decided, she would begin with him, hoping to be able to break the news gently enough to make it acceptable. As overwrought as his mother was, she might better be the last to know, with Blaize and Mark the ones to tell her, once they had learned the truth. But that all hinged on what Blaize did now. If something changed with him, then Samantha's plan would have to change also. Nervously, she awaited Blaize's call. Whatever else happened, there was one question she planned to ask him to remove her last doubts. At last the telephone rang.

'Hello, darling,' she said breathlessly.

'Hello, Samantha,' Blaize said. 'How are you this evening?'

Samantha's heart sank. Something was wrong. All of the warmth was gone from Blaize's voice. He could be talking to a stranger. Getting a tight grip on her quivering nerves, she replied calmly, 'Fine, Blaize. How are you? How is your mother? Was she pleased to hear the news?'

'Oh, yes. Very pleased,' Blaize replied. 'The doctor said she was a hundred per cent better today. He let her come home.'

When Blaize said nothing further for several seconds, Samantha plunged ahead. There was no point in delaying what she knew must be coming.

'Then you'll be able to come out here soon?' she asked, feeling a lead weight settle into her midsection at the sound of Blaize's clearing his throat.

'I'm afraid . . . that something's come up,' he said. 'We're having—er—some financial problems that require my presence in London immediately. I'm not sure when I'll be able to come to California again. I'm sure you understand.'

There was a meaningful, leering note in Blaize's last sentence. What, Samantha wondered, did he think she would understand?

'No, I can't say that I do,' she replied, frowning. 'Do you plan to spend the rest of your life in England?'

'Samantha, don't make this difficult for me,' Blaize's voice said harshly. 'You're not stupid, and neither am I. Let's let it go at that, shall we? If I ever want to see you again, which I doubt, I'll let you know.

There was a click, the dial tone returned, and Samantha was left staring at her receiver, her question unasked, but a million others suddenly racing through her mind. Was this the best Blaize could do at breaking off their love affair? Did he think he could end it like that, with a few terse sentences that implied that she had done something wrong, and he was blameless? Or did he think she had done something? If so, what on earth could it be?

If Blaize had tried to let her down gently, Samantha had been prepared to give him the tongue-lashing of his life, even if she was crying buckets at the same time. As it was, she was left completely up in the air, a rapidly boiling anger overriding the ache in her heart and preventing a single tear from falling.

'I won't put up with this!' she cried, at last banging the receiver into its cradle. 'Even if he doesn't love me, I want to know what in the devil he thinks he's doing, treating me like some criminal. So he doubts he'll ever want to see me again, does he? Well, that's just too damn bad! When he gets back from England, he's going to see me whether he wants to or not!'

'Congreve was right about women,' Bill remarked in the morning, when the still seething Samantha had loudly told him what had happened and exactly what she thought of Blaize Leighton. 'Hell hath no fury like a woman scorned.'

'Not so much scorned as reviled,' Samantha retorted. 'At least that won't be more roses,' she added as her doorbell rang.

'Samantha Bennet? Special delivery,' said the postman who stood before her in the doorway. 'Sign right there.'

Samantha signed and took the envelope, looking curiously at the delicately scrawled address on the heavy, expensive paper. She turned the envelope over. Embossed on the back flap was the return address. The name of the sender was A. M. Leighton.

'Oh, my!' Samantha said, sitting down with a thud on to her favourite cushion. 'I think this is from Blaize's mother. I also think it answers my question that I didn't get to ask. Her initials are A. M.'

'Anne-Marie,' Bill said. 'Yes, I guess it does. Well, for God's sake, woman, don't just look at it, open it!'

With shaking fingers, Samantha tore open the envelope, pulled out the letter, and unfolded it. Lying inside the folded letter was something that made her gasp. 'Oh, my God!' she cried.

'What is it?' Bill jumped to his feet and came to peer over her shoulder. 'Good lord! A cheque for ten thousand dollars. Pick it up. What does she say?'

Samantha took the cheque and laid it aside, then read the short letter.

> My dear Miss Bennet,
>   I don't know how to thank you for your efforts on my behalf, but maybe the enclosed cheque will help a little to convey my gratitude. I have lived for years, dreading that my secret might be revealed. Blaize, of course, must never know. I promised Mr Leighton that I would carry the secret to my grave. Blaize assures me that you are of excellent character. I trust that you will therefore maintain the silence. However, if either you or Mr Westland should happen to think this is an opportunity for blackmail, rest assured that I would not flinch from prosecuting you to the full extent of the law, promise or no.
>
> Sincerely, Anne M Leighton

'Blackmail!' Samantha cried. 'Of all the nerve!' She picked up the cheque, glared at it as if it were a snake, then deliberately tore it into tiny bits and stuffed them back into the envelope with the letter. 'Well, what are you staring at?' she demanded of Bill. 'You didn't expect me to keep it, did you?'

'No,' he said with a sigh, 'but it did look nice.'

'Nice!' Samantha shook her head. If she had felt angry yesterday, she was furious now. She was not going to sit here in her little apartment in Los Angeles, while those nasty Leightons besmirched her character and tore her heart out at the same time. And all the while, poor Mark Westland, who knew nothing of this mess, was being similarly mistreated.

'I'm going to New York,' Samantha announced, getting to her feet. 'I have to find out what's going on with Blaize, and try to get his mother to see things in a different light. She at least ought to be told that Mark has no idea who or where she is.'

'I'm not sure you ought to do that,' Bill said cautiously.

'I'm not either,' Samantha agreed, 'but I'm going to do it anyway. Drive me to the airport, will you?'

'When?'

'Right now. I'll take the first flight I can get,' Samantha replied, picking up her bag. 'Call Mark for me, will you, and tell him I've got a sick cousin or something, and feed the dogs?'

Bill chuckled. 'Sure, but don't you think you'd better change your clothes if you're going to beard Mrs Leighton in her penthouse?'

Samantha glanced down at her faded jeans and baggy sweater and grimaced. 'I suppose so. Wait right here. I'll be ready in ten minutes.'

In ten minutes Samantha was ready, but it was ten hours later, seven allowing for the change in time zones, when she arrived in New York. Her brash con-

fidence had begun to falter en route, and she had had
to give herself a continual pep talk to keep herself
from turning around and catching the next plane back
to Los Angeles. The lights of Manhattan after dark
were intimidating, and she felt very small and in-
secure in the taxi as they sped through mid-town and
on to the exclusive Central Park West address of
A. M. Leighton. She felt drab and insignificant in her
simple navy blue suit as she waited for the doorman
to find out if Mrs Leighton would permit her to come
up. At last he nodded and pointed to the appropriate
elevator, as if actually speaking to her was beneath
him.

When she arrived at the top, Samantha stood in the
elegant mirrored foyer and stared at the door in front
of her, her heart pounding. Should she go through
with it? Maybe she had been too hasty. she might
cause more trouble than she could handle. There was
still time to turn around... No, there wasn't. The door
opened, and a dignified-looking, rotund man looked
at her curiously.

'Miss Bennet?' he enquired.

'Y-yes,' Samantha replied, frozen in her position.

'Please come this way,' the man invited, standing
aside and gesturing, as if hoping that hand signals
might encourage Samantha to move.

Her knees shaking, Samantha followed the man,
who moved ahead of her down a long hallway,
stopping by a closed door, where he tapped three times
and then opened the door, indicating that Samantha
should go through.

Prepared to find herself in a bedroom with a frail
woman in her middle fifties, Samantha took only a
step inside what was not a bedroom at all, but an

elegant, book-lined room, containing several red leather chairs and a huge desk. Her heart stopped. Seated at the desk, then rising politely, was Blaize.

'Wh-what are you doing here?' she demanded, staring at him as he stood frowning down at her, his eyes cold as ice. 'I thought you were in London.' What was wrong with the man? Why was he looking at her like that? And why, oh, why, did her body feel like a quivering mass of jelly as soon as she saw him?

'Obviously,' he said, a nasty little smile curling one side of his mouth upward. 'You wasted precious little time in getting here, once you thought I was gone, did you?'

'What in the devil are you talking about?' Samantha asked, her voice rising.

'Shhh. Not so loud.' Blaize said, shaking his head at her. 'My mother is only two doors away, and I certainly don't plan to let you disturb her further.'

'Disturb her further? I haven't disturbed her at all!' None of this made any sense. Not the slightest, tiniest bit of sense!

'Sit down, Samantha,' Blaize ordered, pointing to a chair. 'I think it's high time you were honest with me, for the first time. I'd at least like the opportunity to admire your cleverness. I must admit, you had me fooled completely.'

Samantha sat, her head spinning. This was worse than Alice in Wonderland, this was Kafka at his most demonic. Where had the soft-voiced Blaize Leighton she loved gone? What did this strange, cold man want to know? Worse yet, it suddenly occurred to her that she might be lucky to get out of this madhouse alive.

'Tell me what you want to know,' she suggested, playing for time and hoping for a clue.

'How about starting when you first decided I was the biggest sucker on the face of the earth?' Blaize replied. 'Was it when I fell in that trench, or the first time I made the mistake of telling you I loved you? Or was it when you conned me into giving money to that old people's home?'

What on earth had made Blaize decide she'd been so devious and deceptive? Samantha wondered, her brow furrowed as she stared at him.

'I can't answer that,' she replied, shaking her head. 'None of your accusations is true. I have no idea why you think I tried to deceive you. Would you mind explaining yourself?'

'Samantha, Samantha,' Blaize said, smiling sadly, 'I can't believe it, even though I'm seeing it. You are really a consummate liar.'

'Liar!' Samantha cried, enraged. How dared this man, who had deceived her so cruelly, call her a liar? 'I am not a liar. You, Mr Leighton, are the world's champion in that department! Thank God I suspected it all along, or I might really have fallen for your romance and roses line.'

Blaize's expression hardened. 'It wasn't a line at the time, Samantha. Unlike you, I never suspected you didn't really care. It wasn't very pleasant to have my illusions shattered so quickly and completely.'

Illusions shattered? 'I'll just bet it wasn't,' Samantha said sarcastically. 'The only illusion you ever had was that I was a complete fool. Now, either tell me what you mean by your insane accusations, or take me to see your mother. I have something important to tell her.'

'I'm sure you do,' Blaize said drily. 'How much do you want this time? Another fifty thousand?'

'Fifty thousand what?' The words were no sooner out than suddenly the light dawned on Samantha. 'Do you mean,' she said very softly, 'that you think I asked your mother for fifty thousand dollars?' She leaped from her chair and leaned on Blaize's desk, her head bent toward him menacingly. 'Is that what you mean?' she shouted.

'You know damn well it is,' Blaize replied, 'and keep your voice down.'

'I will not! I never asked your mother for a penny! Who told you that I did?'

'She did,' Blaize replied calmly. 'Please sit down.'

Samantha did not have to be told. Her knees suddenly lost their strength and she sank into the chair behind her, staring at Blaize while she tried to understand the meaning of what he had told her. Why would his mother tell him such a lie? What did she hope to gain? Did she assume that Samantha knew her secret, and fear that if she and Blaize became close she would tell him what she knew? If so, the poor woman would be terrified for the rest of her life, in spite of her brave threat in her letter. For it was obviously only a threat. Anne-Marie Leighton would go to any lengths to keep Blaize from finding out the truth, even to destroying her son's happiness. Perhaps, Samantha thought sadly, there was even some jealousy here. If Blaize had spoken of his affection for Samantha Bennet, his mother might have thought her a threat in more than one way.

'Puts a rather different light on things, doesn't it?' Blaize said drily, lifting one eyebrow sardonically at Samantha.

'Yes, but not in the way you think,' Samantha replied, chewing her lip thoughtfully. 'It makes me wonder why you were so ready to believe your mother, when you knew perfectly well that I'm not the kind of person who would stoop to such a thing as blackmail. Of course, I understand that one is more inclined to believe one's own parent than a person they've only known a short time. I know I was ready to believe that you might have only been using me to get at Mark Westland's book. I tried very hard to believe that. Right now, I don't know what to believe any more.'

With a tired sigh, Samantha stood up, opened her bag and found the envelope Blaize's mother had sent. She scooped the shredded cheque out and let the pieces cascade down onto Blaize's desk.

'I never asked your mother for any money. She sent me a cheque for ten thousand dollars. I don't want it, or any other cheque. These are the pieces. Glue them back together if you don't believe me. Not that I really care whether you do or not.'

Blaize eyed Samantha suspiciously. 'Then why did you come here tonight?' he asked.

'That,' Samantha replied coldly, 'is something you'll never know. Goodbye, Mr Leighton. I hope I never see you again as long as I live.' With that, she turned and started for the door.

'Samantha, wait!' Blaize called after her.

She paused by the door. 'No, *you* wait,' she said, pointing a staying finger at him as he started towards her. 'Don't come near me. I meant exactly what I said, not something you wanted to hear. There is nothing you could do to undo the damage you've done here tonight. I once thought I loved you, but I was wrong. That was someone else, not a man who could suspect me of blackmailing his mother. If you ever come near me again, I'll be waiting with something a lot more lethal than a baseball bat.'

She fled out the door, slamming it behind her, scarcely breathing until she had reached the pavement in front of the huge old building. 'Thank goodness,' she breathed, as a taxi pulled up to the building to let out some passengers, and responded with a nod as she enquired if he was now free. In a moment she was inside.

'Where to?' the driver asked.

'The airport. Kennedy,' Samantha replied. 'Hurry.' She couldn't get out of New York soon enough. She had to get home before she started to really think about what had happened. Until then, she had to put her mind and body on hold, or they would surely betray her.

CHAPTER NINE

'It is definitely all over now,' Samantha said, staring into her coffee-cup and poking morosely at the pastry the waitress had set before her.

After finding that she did not have enough money for a taxi to her house from Los Angeles International, she had reluctantly called Bill. Now she was glad that she had. In the chilly, early dawn light, Samantha had dreaded returning to her apartment and the ghosts of Blaize Leighton that lived there. Understanding, Bill had stopped at a small, all-night restaurant in a nearby shopping centre and invited her to talk it out for a while.

'I wouldn't make any rash decisions now,' Bill said. 'You're too upset.'

'Rash decisions! I don't think it's rash to not want anything to do with a man who'd accuse you of blackmailing his mother. No, Bill, this is it.' It was the only sensible decision. Samantha had told herself over and over on the plane home. The only intelligent one.

'You might try looking at it from Leighton's point of view,' Bill suggested gently.

'I did,' Samantha replied, scowling. 'I can see why he'd believe his mother, at first. But you'd think he'd at least have some second thoughts, wouldn't you? And why are you defending him? You should be glad I'm through with Blaize Leighton.'

Bill shrugged. 'I would be, if I thought you were, and if I thought it would make you happier in the end. But I'm afraid I don't have any illusions on either score. I want you to be happy, Sam. That's all.'

Samantha bit her lip. She didn't deserve a friend as good and kind as Bill.

'You're too good to be true, Bill Grimes,' she said, 'and I really appreciate it. But I still say I don't want to see Blaize again. I need to brace myself for one last good cry, and then start life all over, as if Blaize Leighton never existed.'

'What if he decides to believe you now, instead of his mother, and starts in with the roses again? You said he claimed he really did love you before his mother pulled the rug out from under him.'

'He'd better not try it,' Samantha said, setting her jaw stubbornly. 'The first thing I'm going to do is get an unlisted telephone number. If he tries sending flowers, I'll simply tell the florist to take them directly to Shady Oaks.'

'And if he comes pounding on your door?'

'I won't let him in and I won't talk to him. I'll call the police if I have to,' Samantha replied, although the thought of having to do any such thing made her feel physically ill.

'There's one other possibility you may have overlooked,' Bill said.

'What's that?'

'He might decide to go and see Mark Westland.'

Samantha stared at Bill. 'Oh, lord, that's right. I'd almost forgotten . . . well, I can't help it if he does! Do you think Mark would guess the truth right away?'

'I don't know,' Bill replied, looking thoughtful. 'It might take him a little while to put it all together, and then again it might hit him immediately, like a ton of bricks. I'd certainly like to be a mouse in the corner when it happened. Especially since my ability to administer first aid could come in very handy. I don't know how good Mark's heart is, but he is seventy years old.'

'Oh, drat!' Samantha cried. 'Then I couldn't let Blaize go to see him, if there was any way to stop him, could I?' She paused and frowned as Bill shook his head in reply. 'You know,' she said, 'I'll bet that's one of the reasons Anne-Marie Leighton made those accusations about me. She wanted to keep Blaize away from here so he wouldn't be likely to meet Mark. Poor woman. I wonder what she'll do if Blaize did believe me, and asks her why she did what she did?'

'You'll probably find out,' Bill replied with a wry smile. 'Well, are you ready to go home and face your ghosts? I think they'll probably become material before the day is over.'

'That soon?' Samantha croaked.

'That soon,' Bill replied.

'I wish I was dead,' Samantha said sadly. 'No, I don't. I wish I hadn't gone to New York. Why didn't I leave well enough alone?'

'That's never been your strong point,' Bill said with a smile.

'It certainly hasn't,' Samantha agreed, wishing fervently that it had. If it had, she'd still be doing routine stories for some newspaper, and would never have met either Mark Westland or Blaize Leighton.

Slim and Poco were so glad to see their wandering mistress that for a while Samantha was distracted from her problems and, except for fatigue from lack of sleep, felt almost normal. She made arrangements to have her telephone number changed and unlisted, and breathed a sigh of relief when it was time to go to her usual appointment with Mark Westland and there had been no floral assaults. Maybe Bill was wrong. Maybe Blaize was still convinced of Samantha Bennet's treachery and would never return again. After all, his mother had convinced him once. She might be able to do so again.

The sight of the handsome old actor was almost too much for Samantha's exhausted nerves. It seemed as if, for her, the similarities between Mark and Blaize were somehow enhanced. Mark's every gesture and expression reminded her of Blaize.

'Is something bothering you, Samantha?' Mark Westland asked, when she had to ask him to repeat several sentences after discovering she had forgotten to turn on her tape recorder. 'You look very tired. Are you and young Leighton at odds again?'

'Oh, no!' Samantha replied quickly. 'He's in New York right now, and I miss him. That's all.'

Mark smiled. 'You're a terrible liar, Samantha,' he said gently. 'Blaize called me this morning when he found you'd gotten an unlisted telephone number. He'd called your friend Grimes, who told him you were adamant about not wanting to see him again, and he wasn't sure how stubborn you might be. Blaize told me what happened last night. It's certainly a shame about his mother. I wonder what she thinks that I know?' When Samantha only smiled weakly and gave a little shrug, he shook his head and then went on, 'Anyway, Blaize asked my opinion on whether there was any chance you'd ever forgive him. I told him I thought you were a very fair person and that you probably would at least hear him out. You will, won't you?'

The tears that Samantha had not had time for started to fill her eyes, but she blinked them back. So Blaize had decided he believed her side of the story. He wanted her to forgive him for being such an unreasonable beast. And doubtless it also meant he would be coming to try and see her, just as Bill had predicted. Well, he could just stay in New York! She was far from ready to listen to Blaize Leighton.

'I don't know!' she said sharply. 'And I don't know why everyone seems to be on Blaize's side. All I hear is "listen to his side of it, look at his viewpoint." How about mine? I don't like being called a blackmailer. I don't know if I'll listen or not. Ever!'

'I hope you do.' Mark cocked his head and studied Samantha thoughtfully, a smile quirking his mouth in a manner that looked so much like Blaize that Samantha quickly looked away. As if one of her problems weren't enough, she thought bitterly.

'I'll think about it,' she replied. 'Now, let's get back to that senator who thought you were romancing his daughter. Did he really challenge you to a duel with swords?'

'He really did. One more thing about Blaize Leighton. The next time he's out here, bring him to meet me, will you? I'd like to see this young man who's causing you to lose so much sleep.'

Samantha could only nod and bite her lip. Mark Westland was using the same kind of trick that Blaize did, ignoring the fact that she might not even talk to Blaize, and asking her to bring him to his house. Whether she actually did so or not was going to depend on a great many things, only the first of which was any decision she might make about talking to Blaize again.

By the time she got home, Samantha was so tired that she felt as if her very bones ached. Small wonder, she thought, for she had slept only a couple of hours last night. She needed some rest before she tried to decide what to do about Blaize Leighton or anything else. She dropped her bag and briefcase by her kitchen door, fed her dogs, swallowed a glass of milk, and then lay down on her sofa. She turned on her television, but fell asleep before the nightly newscaster had finished his first gloomy item for the day. When she awoke, it was dark, the only illumination in the room from an old John Wayne movie on the television.

Samantha stared at the picture for a few minutes, feeling uneasy. Something was different. What was it? She blinked sleepily and closed her eyes again. She wasn't awake yet, that was all. Or her eyes were playing tricks on her. There wasn't any bouquet of roses on top of her television set. She had taken them all to Shady Oaks Rest Home on Saturday, hadn't she? She opened her eyes again. The bouquet was still there, huge and fresh-looking, the roses almost black in the dim light. Could it have been there when she got home and she was too tired to have noticed it? Bill might have brought it in. He had a key. She pushed herself up on to her elbows and frowned. Something felt wrong. Almost as if there were someone else in the room, watching her. Cautiously she looked around, first towards her kitchen and then back towards her front door. Suddenly her heart stopped and she let out a little gasp. There, sprawled in her black bean-bag chair, his dark trousers and sweater making him almost invisible, was Blaize.

'Hello, Samantha,' he said softly. 'Sorry to startle you like that.'

'Blaize! How did you get in here?' she cried, swinging her feet quickly to the floor and pushing her hair back from her face. Her mind exploded with un-asked questions and her body began to tremble viol-ently. What was he doing, sitting there in her chair so quietly, watching her like that? Why had he come? And why couldn't she move? All she could do was stare at him, her eyes locked on to his, which seemed to flicker with a light of their own in the semi-darkness.

'I borrowed Bill's key,' Blaize answered, his slanted smile quirking upwards. 'I wasn't sure you'd let me in, otherwise.'

'B-but when? How?' Samantha asked stupidly, gesturing toward her dogs, sleeping quietly at Blaize's feet. 'Didn't those dummies even bark, or did I sleep right through their racket?'

Blaize shook his head, still smiling. 'I was here when you got home. You didn't come upstairs. I'd gone up to the bath, saw your nice, comfortable-looking bed, and lay down and fell asleep. I didn't sleep much last night, either. When I woke up, you were sound asleep down here, so I sat down to wait for you to waken again. I've been dozing off and on myself. Do you suppose we could talk now? It doesn't look as if you're going to throw me out or take your baseball bat to me.'

Samantha opened her mouth, but no words formed from the scramble of thoughts in her head. It was just as well. None of them made any sense, anyway, any more than the way she was feeling. At first she had felt a cold sort of fear at the sight of Blaize, but now she was so warm that her upper lip was perspiring. Some kind of glow from Blaize had come inside her and made her that way. She cleared her throat, trying desperately to erase thoughts of roses and kisses and strong, gentle arms, and remember what she had planned to say if she ever did say anything to this man again.

'Do you want to talk?' Blaize repeated, when Samantha still remained silent. 'If you'd rather go back to sleep, I'll wait.'

'I...no. What do you want to talk about?' Samantha finally got out, blushing as Blaize burst out laughing.

'I'm sorry,' he said, still chuckling, 'but you look like an adorable little sleepy owl sitting there. I do love you, Samantha. Maybe you should just listen while I apologise for an hour or two. How would that be?'

'No!' Samantha jumped to her feet and quickly turned on some lights. 'I don't want to hear your apology. It's too late. What you did was unforgivable.' She turned her back on Blaize and hurried into her kitchen, trying to ignore echoes of Mark's voice saying that she'd be fair and listen. She felt dizzy. Probably, she reasoned, because she hadn't eaten. She jerked open her refrigerator and stared inside. 'Darn it, there's nothing to eat! I didn't get any dinner at all.'

'I'm hungry, too,' Blaize said, following her into the kitchen. 'Why don't we send out for a pizza? I won't apologise. I'll just tell you what happened and let you draw your own conclusions about how wrong I was.'

Samantha slammed her refrigerator door with unnecessary force, and turned back to Blaize. 'No! I don't want you here,' she said. Her heart was pounding at a terrific speed, and she leaned back against the refrigerator to try to eliminate the sense of vertigo that was creeping up on her. She swallowed hard, watching as Blaize studied her face, his own look guarded but not unfriendly. Damn the man! Just his being here, looking, in the small brightly lit room, so tall and solid and strong and good, was eroding her resolve away in huge chunks. She swayed suddenly and clutched at the refrigerator door-handle for support.

'I don't think you're quite sure of that,' Blaize said, coming quickly to her side and putting his hands on her shoulders. 'I also think you'd better sit down before you fall down. When was the last time you ate?' As he said this, he pulled out a chair and gently propelled her into it.

'I don't remember,' Samantha said crossly, feeling control of the situation slipping from her grasp. ' I don't care what you think. I still don't...'

'Shhh,' Blaize interrupted, putting a finger to his lips, and then smiling. 'I'll call the fastest pizza place around and at least solve one of your problems for you. Do you want one with everything on it?'

'I don't want any!' Samantha cried, jumping to her feet. The sudden motion was too much for her hungry, anguished body. Stars danced before her eyes and a black wave started to engulf her.

'Samantha!'

She heard Blaize's cry, felt his arms go around her, then felt the black wave recede.

'I-I'm all right,' she said hoarsely, her eyes meeting those deep, velvet-brown eyes that were now only inches from her own.

'No, you're not,' Blaize said, frowning severely. 'You stay put in that chair or I'll tie you to it. Do you hear me?'

'All right.' Samantha sat quietly, watching as Blaize found a number and placed his call. 'Tell them to hold the anchovies,' she said.

Blaize raised one eyebrow at her, smiled, and nodded.

While Blaize placed the order, Samantha stared at him, trying to make some sense of the way she was feeling now. Her baseball bat was still behind the curtains, right next to where Blaize was standing, but she knew she could never use it or anything else to harm him. She couldn't bear the thought of him being hurt, by her or anyone else. Did she really want him to go? He said he loved her. There was no reason for him to be here now if he didn't.

Deep inside, Samantha felt something warm and good begin to form as Blaize finished his call and came to sit opposite her at the table. He leaned his chin on his hand and smiled.

'Help is on the way,' he said. 'Shall we talk about the weather until it gets here?'

He looks so much like Mark, Samantha thought, a little ache forming a twin beside the happier spot in her heart. If he were in the movies, every woman in the world would fall in love with him. As it was, *she* was in love with him, so deeply that now it seemed his accusations of the night before were only a bad dream. Still, she needed to know why he had made them. Perhaps there would be something there to help her decide how she could tell him what she knew of his real beginnings, if indeed she ever could. But if she loved him, somehow she would have to find a way. Did she even dare to love him?

'You can go ahead and tell me what happened,' she said quietly. 'I'll listen.'

Blaize rubbed his forehead and looked down at his hands. 'Well, first of all,' he said slowly, 'I should tell you that, from the first time I mentioned my interest in you to my mother, she seemed unusually reserved about it. I say that,' he added, glancing up at Samantha with a rueful smile, 'because she's been trying to get me married off for years, and usually tries to promote anyone I show interest in who isn't the two-headed lady from the circus. By last week, as her heart condition worsened, I had gathered that it was somehow linked to my interest in you as much as it was to Mark Westland's book, although when I asked her directly she denied it.

'I actually felt I had to sneak off to come out here for that short visit on Friday night, so that she wouldn't know. I hated that feeling, but I was sure that, once she knew you had taken care of her worries about Mark's memoirs, she'd feel differently about you. But, as you probably can guess, she didn't. As soon as I told her that, and about what was in those notes I sent with your flowers last week, she became almost hysterical. That's when she told me that you had been deceiving me all along, that you'd demanded money from her a long time ago, and that after my visit you'd called her again. She said this time she gave in and agreed, if you would promise never to see me again as well as promising to keep Mark's story quiet.

'Naturally, I was thunderstuck by what she said, but it didn't occur to me that she would make up such a story. I thought of calling you to ask you what you had to say for yourself, but somehow I couldn't bring myself to do that. I felt too miserable. All I could think to do was to tell you goodbye, and let you know I'd found out about your little game. I did think your response was a little strange, but marked it up to your ability to play your part to perfection. And that, my love, is all there is to tell, unless you want the apology that goes with it, which includes the fact that as soon as you started yelling at me last night I knew I'd been a perfect fool to believe you could have done such a thing.'

He smiled crookedly at Samantha, and for the first time she was able to smile back.

'Not quite perfect,' she said. 'I claim that title for having doubted you all along. I guess I couldn't quite believe a person could be so positive about being in love so fast. I never met anyone before who was.' And now I've met two, she thought. You and your father. She sighed and bit her lip. There still was nothing to go on about how to tell him. She didn't even know if he'd told his mother about his latest change of heart.

'Did you tell your mother you no longer believed I'd tried to blackmail her?' she asked.

Blaize nodded, his mouth twisting into a grimace as he did so. 'I didn't even get around to asking her why she'd sent you that cheque. When I told her I didn't believe her story, and was coming to beg your forgiveness, she did become hysterical, making wild accusations and carrying on about what a devil Mark

Westland is and how you must be one too, for working with him. She screamed that I must never see either one of you, as long as I lived. I had to call the doctor and have her sedated. She's going to be under a psychiatrist's care for some time, I'm afraid.'

'Oh, Blaize, I'm so sorry.' Samantha reached over to place her hand on his. 'Do you have any idea what it is that she's so afraid of having disclosed?' she asked, although she knew that he could not.

'Not the slightest,' Blaize confirmed. 'God knows I've tried to find out. She seemed to think you knew, but after this last outburst I'm inclined to think it's some fabrication she's allowed to take over her mind. Has Mark actually told you something that she might not want revealed?'

Samantha took a deep breath and crossed her fingers tightly beneath the table to steel her nerves against betraying the magnitude of her secret. 'Yes,' she answered slowly and calmly, 'but I'm not at liberty to tell you about it yet. I will as soon as I can, though. I promise.' There. She had committed herself. Now the only questions were how and when and where.

'Why the mystery?' Blaize asked, frowning. 'I'm not a naive child, you know. I doubt anything either of my parents did would shock me that much.'

Little do you know, Samantha thought, raising her eyebrows and giving Blaize a rueful smile. 'Let me be the judge of that,' she said. 'Please don't press me on it right now.'

Fortunately, at that moment the doorbell rang, announcing the arrival of the pizza man, and Blaize went to the door, returning with a huge box and a bag containing drinks, a container of salad and several apple tarts.

While they ate, conversation between them was limited, and very non-emotional. When they had finished, Samantha stood up to clear the dishes away. She had scarcely begun when Blaize came up behind her and took the dishes from her hands, then turned her to face him.

'I've kept my hands off of you as long as I can,' he said huskily. 'If you've accepted my explanation, as I think you have, can we go back and start again where we left off last Friday? At the point where you told me you loved me?'

Samantha looked into that dear, loving smile, a mist of tears coming to her eyes. They could never really go back to that point, given what she knew now, but she loved Blaize so. She wanted him to be absolutely sure of that now.

'I do love you,' she said. 'Very much.' She flung her arms around him and held him close, her cheek pressed against his chest, revelling in the feeling of warmth and security it gave as his arms closed around her and his hand gently stroked her hair.

Slowly, he put his hand on her cheek and raised her face to his, his lips finding hers and pressing into them with a passion that set Samantha's heart singing wildly, her tongue frantically trying to keep pace and capture Blaize's as it darted around her mouth on a mission of wild but delicious torment. Finally he raised his head, his eyes so dark with love and desire that Samantha felt herself shiver with answering longings. He smiled, and she smiled in return.

'Have you given any positive thoughts to what I asked in those notes?' he asked, his fingers caressing beneath her chin. 'I didn't find them under your pillow, but I thought perhaps you'd thrown them out when you were so angry.'

Samantha blushed, a damper falling on her feelings of joy. Now she had to tell him the truth about that, and it was not going to be pleasant.

'I'm afraid it's time for my confession and apology,' she said in a small voice. 'When you asked me on Friday to talk to Mark, I thought it meant that was your main motive in everything you'd done. I was so stupid. But I was also very upset, because I knew I'd fallen in love with you. So, when the roses came, I threw the notes out without reading them, and then took the flowers to Shady Oaks. I'm afraid you'll have to tell me what they said.'

Blaize shook his head, pretending to give Samantha a severe frown and then bursting into laughter. 'I think it's just as well. I'd rather ask you in person, anyway. Will you marry me?'

'Will I . . . ?' Samantha's eyes grew wide. 'That was in those notes? But if I'd read them, then I wouldn't have thought . . . but then, when you suspected me of blackmail, it would have been even worse, wouldn't it?'

'I think it would,' Blaize replied, nodding soberly. 'Well, what do you think? Will you come to the most beautiful church in New England, filled with flowers, and come down the aisle to me, the most beautiful bride in the world?'

Samantha blinked. Oh, lord, she might have known Blaize would want a very big, romantic wedding! Somehow, the thought terrified her, but she could probably get used to the idea. However, there was still the problem of when to tell him her secret. Was it possible that might upset him so much he would want to reconsider his proposal? She had better make sure first. For now, the answer would have to be tentative.

'I'm inclined to say yes,' she replied, smiling mischievously to remove any hurt there might be in her reply, 'but I have to think it over for a little while. It is rather sudden, you know. Only this morning I was trying to convince myself I didn't want to see you again. Let me settle down a bit.'

'You are a very wise woman,' Blaize said, hugging her tightly. 'Also, I imagine, still very tired. Do you suppose we might sneak upstairs to that nice bed of yours and spend what's left of the night there?'

'Sleeping?' Samantha asked, lifting her eyebrows at Blaize.

'Some of the time,' he replied, imitating her raised eyebrows and grinning with devilish delight.

'I think that sounds like a wonderful idea,' she said, squealing as Blaize immediately swept her into his arms. Perhaps, she thought, getting rid of the sexual tension that had been building between them for so long would get her ready for revealing her secret, or at least make her forget it temporarily.

'I'm not very experienced at this,' Samantha said, eyeing Blaize apprehensively.

'Don't worry,' he replied, laying her gently on the bed, then stretching out beside her and tucking her head on to his shoulder. 'I wouldn't be here if I thought you were. Those coy, silly games that experienced women play turn me off completely.' He snuggled her against him and kissed her lips very softly, nibbling around their edges, along her cheeks and chin.

Samantha closed her eyes, dreamily losing herself in the sensations that began flooding her being. There was the warmth of Blaize's lips, a warmth that seemed to start a fire wherever they touched. There was the scent of him that filled her nostrils, a combination of heather and spice and musky masculinity that was intoxicating. Her hand stole behind his neck, feeling the smooth skin and then the thick, dark curls that were soft and yet springy and vital. When he pressed his body against hers, she tightened her own hold, feeling as if there were no way on earth she could be close enough to him. His hand stole between them, and she relinquished her grasp to permit its explorations. Very delicately he placed his hand over first one breast and then the other, a little sigh coming from him as she pressed against his hand.

'Do you mind?' he asked against her lips as his fingers began to unfasten her blouse.

'No, do you?' Samantha replied, beginning to pull Blaize's sweater up, then inserting her hand beneath it and sliding it across his bare back.

Blaize's answer was an 'Mmmm' of pleasure.

Very slowly, he unfastened Samantha's blouse, so slowly that she was tempted to help him. Every place his fingers touched her bare skin came alive. When at last he slipped the blouse from her, she gave a sigh of relief and smiled when he drew his head back and cocked a questioning eyebrow at her.

'Impatient?' he asked.

'Yes,' she answered, helping him remove his sweater. There, before her at last, was the chest with the moderate amount of hair and the mole on his left shoulder. 'It's not as large as I imagined,' she said, touching it with one finger. Suddenly she remembered something else and smiled again. 'At last I will get to see that scar,' she said, reaching for the buckle on Blaize's belt.

'Not so fast, my love,' Blaize said, removing her eager fingers. 'Let's get even first.' He unfastened her bra and tossed it aside. 'That's better,' he said, his eyes feasting on her warm curves. He pulled her back against him, starting a series of kisses with her lips once again, then down her throat, so delicately that Samantha scarcely could feel them, and yet felt inside as if a million wild birds were flying in soaring circles, carrying her with them ever higher. As his lips reached the rosy peaks of her breasts, his hand cupped beneath to hold his quarry. A moan escaped Samantha's lips and her hands gripped tightly on the firm muscles of Blaize's shoulders. She had never felt anything so electric in her life. Every cell in her body must be pulsing with a strange new rhythm. She wanted Blaize's body close to her as she wanted food when she was starving. When his hand started to unfasten her slacks, she drew in her breath sharply. She needed him to touch her where her longing was most intense. She felt she could scarcely wait another moment. When Blaize drew back, she stared at him in confusion.

'What's wrong?' she asked.

'Not a thing,' he replied. 'I've just never figured out how a person could get a pair of slacks off another person with only one hand, especially when they're wriggling like you are.' He grinned as Samantha frowned, and turned so that he could use both hands. 'Don't worry, it won't go away,' he said. 'It will get even better, I promise.' He pulled Samantha's slacks off and then looked at her pink and white bikinis thoughtfully. 'Shall we leave those on for a while?' he asked.

Samantha started to frown, then caught the twinkle in Blaize's eyes and laughed instead. 'You are a tease, Blaize Leighton,' she said. 'I think I'll put my clothes back on and go and talk to my dogs.' She rose up on one elbow, but Blaize firmly pushed her back down.

'Oh, no, you won't,' he replied. He whisked Samantha's bikinis off. 'Now it's your turn again,' he said, kneeling beside her, 'if you're sure you're ready for this to go all the way. I'll wait until we're married, if you'd prefer, and we can just do some petting and snuggling now.'

'You really mean that, don't you?' Samantha said softly. She had never imagined that a man could be as gentle and loving and considerate as Blaize was. It made her want to belong to him completely all the more.

'Sure as my name's Blaize Leighton,' he replied, smiling down at her. 'I want to spend my life making you happy in every way, my love, but that doesn't mean I can't wait a little longer to give you the ultimate pleasure. There are many other ways to make love, you know.'

Sure as his name was Blaize Leighton. Samantha felt as if her heart would break from the sudden pain that shot through her. She had to tell him the secret, and she had to tell him now. She pursed her mouth and swallowed hard.

'I want you,' she said hoarsely. 'I want you now and I want you more than I ever dreamed I could want any man, but there's something I have to tell you first.'

'Samantha, darling, what is it?' Blaize asked anxiously, bending to caress her cheek with a large, warm hand. 'Have you some problem about having children, or some illness...'

'Oh, no! Nothing like that,' Samantha said quickly. She sat up and took Blaize's face between her hands, her eyes scanning his beloved features soberly. 'Nothing like that at all. I'm in perfect health and I want a dozen children. It has to do with your mother's secret. I think I should tell you now.' She looked down at her naked body and smiled wryly. 'But maybe not like this. Just stay right here while I put on my caftan.'

'I don't understand,' Blaize said, watching as Samantha went to her wardrobe, took out her caftan, and slipped it over her head. 'What could that possibly have to do with us?'

Samantha glanced in her mirror, picked up her brush and gave a quick smoothing to her hair. Don't lose your nerve now, she told herself, watching her hand tremble as she put the brush down again.

'Maybe not very much,' she said, turning back toward Blaize, 'and maybe a lot. I'm not sure.' She went back to the bed, where Blaize was sitting cross-legged, wearing only his slacks. She arranged some pillows behind him. 'There,' she said, taking a cross-legged position beside him. 'Brace yourself, my darling. This is quite a story. First, let me tell you the only story Mark Westland really knows about the Leightons.' Quickly, she told Blaize of Mark's episode with the older Leighton.

'That's all he knows?' Blaize asked, puzzled.

'Absolutely. He's as puzzled as I used to be about why your mother is so obsessed with such a trivial event.'

'As you *used* to be?' Blaize cocked his head and looked intently at Samantha. 'You know something more?'

Samantha nodded and rubbed her eyes. She had to keep going now. She had to speak calmly and clearly and keep her thoughts in order. She looked down, then decided it was best to look Blaize straight in the eyes while she told him the rest, no matter how hard it might be.

'It's hard to know where to begin,' she said. 'I guess the next thing is to tell you the story that Mark told me when he got me to confess that I doubted your declarations of love. You see, he, too, believes in love at first sight. It happened to him, once, quite long ago. He was in France, making a movie.' Samantha repeated Mark's story to Blaize, omitting the name of Mark's great love. 'He had tears in his eyes when he finished,' she said. 'He plans to dedicate the book to her, in hopes of finding her again, and his son.'

Deep in Blaize's dark eyes was the flickering of some strong emotion.

'You said the girl only gave her first name,' he said, a strangely hollow sound to his voice. 'Do you know what it was?'

'Anne-Marie,' Samantha replied. She watched a torrent of emotions flash through Blaize's eyes.

'Are you saying that I am Mark Westland's son?' he demanded. He did not wait for Samantha's reply but went on, 'That's impossible! I was named after my father!' He took hold of Samantha's shoulders and shook her. 'That's crazy! How could you come up with something like that? It's only a coincidence that my mother's name is Anne-Marie.'

'Your mother's name was the last thing I found out,' Samantha said, trying to keep her demeanour perfectly calm. 'I noticed almost immediately that you look something like Mark Westland does, even now. Then, when I saw his very first movie...well, it was so obvious that I almost fainted. Bill saw it, too. In fact, he helped me figure out how it all fitted together, so he knows everything, too. Let me tell you what we thought, and try to think of any facts you might know that would help. All right?' She smiled and laid her hand against Blaize's hot cheek, but he brushed it away.

'Sure. Tell me your little fantasy,' he snapped. 'But don't expect me to believe it.'

'I was afraid you might feel that way,' Samantha said with a sigh. 'I don't blame you at all.' She recounted the conversation that she and Bill had had while watching *Nights of Romance*.

'That does have a certain warped logic,' Blaize said when she had finished, 'and Mother does speak French like a native. She went to one of those exclusive girls' schools where they spend half their time in Europe. She might have been in France about then, I don't know. But it still doesn't prove I'm Mark Westland's son.'

'Let's go downstairs,' Samantha suggested. 'You can see that movie and the note your mother wrote when she sent me the cheque.' She got up and held out her hand to Blaize. 'Please?'

Blaize shrugged and ignored her hand, but he got up, tossing his sweater around his bare shoulders, and following her.

'I'll show you part of the movie first,' Samantha said, 'because I saw it and knew before I even got your mother's note.'

Blaize watched silently while Samantha put the tape in her VCR, and then came to sit beside him.

'He's not in this first part,' Samantha said, accelerating the tape for a while. 'Here we are. He'll be along in a few minutes.' She leaned back and watched Blaize's face while he looked at the audition scene featuring the other two actors. Suddenly he leaned forward, staring intently at the picture.

'Give me that,' he said abruptly, taking the control box from Samantha. She looked towards the set and saw that he was looking at the same close-up that had convinced her and Bill.

'My God!' he said softly. 'It's almost like looking in a mirror.' He looked towards Samantha, but seemed to be seeing something far away. 'That would explain so many things,' he murmured. He put the control box down and buried his face in his hands. A moment later, he jumped to his feet and began pacing up and down, his head down and his hands thrust deep in his pockets.

Unwilling to interrupt his thoughts, Samantha sat immobile, her heart going out to him, but not knowing what to do or say to help. He was mumbling as he walked, but she could only hear a few words, and they made no sense. 'Lousy', 'devil', and 'bastard' seemed to recur quite often.

'Do you want to see your mother's note?' Samantha asked at last.

'No!' Blaize roared. 'I'm damned if I do.'

'Then maybe I should tell you that she promised George Leighton to carry the secret to her grave.

Somehow I didn't think I could do that, but maybe I should have.'

'Yes, maybe you should.' Blaize shook his head and buried his face in his hands. 'It fits. Oh, lord, how it all fits.' At last he jerked his head up, pulled on his sweater, and turned towards Samantha.

'I don't know what the hell to do or think,' he said. 'I need some time alone to figure this all out. I don't even know who I really am any more. I'll go down to Malibu for the night, and I'll call you tomorrow.'

Samantha nodded. 'I understand.' She started to rise but, before she was on her feet, Blaize had gone, slamming the door behind him.

With a tired sigh, Samantha sank back down, tears filling her eyes. She should never have told him. She could have told Mark and told him of Anne-Marie's promise to her husband. He might have been content just to know where and who they were. But that didn't seem right, somehow. Blaize's poor mother would go on and on in her terrible state of anxiety. Besides, Blaize was no fool. When he met Mark, as he doubtless would have done quite soon, he would have begun to suspect. No, she had done the right thing, even if it hadn't turned out very well. If only Blaize hadn't stormed off like that. If only he'd let her help him through this. She was going to be his wife, wasn't she?

CHAPTER TEN

'YOU'RE darned right, I am,' Samantha answered herself aloud. 'I'm not going to sit here blubbering. He needs me! *I* know who he is. He's Blaize Leighton, the romantic idiot that I love!'

Samantha got to her feet and dashed up the stairs. In only a few minutes she had dressed in her lovely white dress and tossed a few extra items of clothing into a small suitcase. She hurried back downstairs, took the bouquet of roses from the top of her television set and wrapped it in a swathe of tissue. 'Come on, you two,' she said to her dogs. 'I don't know how soon I'll be back.' She shooed the dogs into the back seat of her car, placed the roses on the front seat beside her, and then smiled wryly to herself. 'Let's hope the police don't stop me for anything. They'd think I'm crazy,' she said. 'Now let's hope I can find Blaize's house without too much trouble.'

It was foggy near the ocean, but at last Samantha found the private road that led to several lovely beachfront homes. Blaize's car identified his, and she parked behind it in his drive, picked up the roses, and went to his door. She raised her hand to ring the bell, then stopped and took a deep breath, trying to still the pounding of her heart. She was not going to let him turn her away, she was not! she resolved for what seemed like the hundredth time. She tucked the roses behind her back with one hand, raised her other hand again and pushed the bell firmly. After a very long pause, during which she felt her knees begin to shake, the door opened.

'Mr Blaize Leighton?' she said to the hollow-eyed man before her. 'My name is Samantha Bennet. I'd like to talk to you, and I brought you these.' She held the bouquet of roses out towards Blaize, her heart sinking at the cold way he stared at them. She re-gathered her courage. 'You don't need to say you don't want any and slam the door in my face, because I don't give up easily, either. May I come in?'

Blaize's expression softened just a trifle. He nodded and stood aside.

'What did you want to say?' he asked.

Samantha frowned. Blaize certainly wasn't making this any easier. He seemed to think he was the only one having a rough night.

'Maybe I should have brought my baseball bat instead,' she muttered. When Blaize only lifted one eyebrow in response, she lifted her chin and plunged ahead. 'I came to tell you that, as far as I can tell, you are still George Blaize Leighton, Jr, and, unless you've changed your mind, I am soon going to be *Mrs* George Blaize Leighton, Jr. As such, I plan to be by your side when you have a problem, not sitting at home, waiting for you to call me when you're through solving it all by yourself. Now, if you've changed your mind, tell me and I'll go away. I'm warning you, though, that this is the last and only time I'll make this offer. There aren't enough roses on earth to get me to go through this again, no matter how much I love you.'

She watched anxiously as Blaize closed his eyes for a moment and seemed to be trying to make himself shake off the tension which had deepened the lines in his face. He tilted his head back and opened his eyes just enough to look at her from beneath his long lashes.

'You are saying a firm yes to marrying me?' he asked, raising his eyebrows questioningly.

'I am,' Samantha replied. 'Very firm.'

Suddenly, all of the tension left Blaize's face, and he smiled, the change from bleak coldness to warmth almost taking Samantha's breath away.

'Then what do I care about anything else?' Blaize reached out and enfolded Samantha in his arms, pressing her close against him. 'And I thought once that you were the one who needed lessons in the meaning of love,' he said, a soft edge of laughter in his voice. 'I'm not sure I deserve you, but how very glad I am that I have you. Shall we go back to bed and start over from where you said that you had something to tell me? We can worry about the rest of it tomorrow.'

'A wonderful idea,' Samantha replied, burrowing close against Blaize's chest. 'First, let me get Slim and Poco. I was hoping you'd want me to stay, so I brought them along.'

'Good. Now the whole family's together,' Blaize said, his smile wide and adoring as he tilted Samantha's face up to receive his kiss.

It was afternoon when Blaize and Samantha finally dressed and took the dogs out for a walk along the beach. Making love, sleeping, then making love again had left them both so joyously happy that they could scarcely take their eyes off one another, hardly bear not to be touching.

'If only Mark and your mother can feel even a little
bit like this,' Samantha said, when finally they agreed
to discuss that difficult problem, sitting nestled
together on a lounge chair on the deck of Blaize's
Malibu home, watching the surf roll in. 'Do you think
it's possible?'

Blaize sighed and tightened his arms around
Samantha. 'If I can get through to Mother that Mark
never knew who she really was there's a chance. I think
Bill must be right, that she thought that my . . . my
other father had told him. I'd better try that before
we approach Mark, don't you think? Besides,' he
smiled ruefully, 'it will give me a little longer to get
used to the idea of meeting my real father. After all
these years, I wouldn't want to let him down by acting
awkward and foolish.'

Samantha took Blaize's face between her hands and
studied it, biting her lip thoughtfully. He was so dear.
Mark was going to be so proud to have him for a son.
After all these years . . .

'I think,' she said slowly, 'that we ought to tell
Mark, that you ought to meet him, as soon as possible. You'll feel a little strange, no matter how long
you wait. But he's an elderly man and, to him, every
day means so much. Finding you will be such a
treasure. He'll understand about waiting for you to
see your mother before he does. I know he will. And
I think it will make it easier for you to face your
mother, when you've met Mark and found out what
a fine man he is.'

'All right,' Blaize agreed, his voice barely audible.
'What do you suggest we do? Go and see him today?'

'Yes.' Samantha nodded. 'I'll call and tell him I'm
coming today, after all, that I have something special

to tell him. You can come along and wait in the car until I've prepared him to meet you.'

It was a scant two hours later when, on the patio behind his home, Mark Westland greeted a very nervous Samantha with a knowing smile.

'And what is this special something you have to tell me?' he asked. 'Have you finally come to your senses about young Leighton? Is there a wedding in your future?'

Samantha blushed. 'Yes,' she answered, then gasped as Mark enveloped her in a bearhug. 'But that's not what I came to tell you,' she added, when he had released her. 'It's something even better.'

'Better?' Mark's eyebrows, twins of Blaize's shot up. 'What could be better than that?'

Oh, lord, I hope I'm doing this right, Samantha thought, swallowing the lump in her throat and taking a deep breath to try to still her trembling. 'How about,' she replied, licking her parched lips, 'finding out that I've found your son and Anne-Marie?'

Mark Westland paled. 'Samantha, that's not something to joke about,' he said severely. He peered into Samantha's wide eyes. 'You're not joking,' he said. Very quickly, he sat down. 'Where are they? Who are they? How did you find them?' he asked in rapid succession.

'She's quite a detective,' came Blaize's voice, and Samantha whirled around.

'Blaize!' she cried. 'You were supposed to wait!'

But her words were lost on the two men. Blaize stepped forward, and Mark jumped to his feet. For a few seconds they stared at each other, each man's face incredulous at the recognition of the likeness between them. Then, drawn together as if by some powerful force, they reached for each other, their embrace so spontaneous, so loving, that tears of happiness for them streamed unchecked down Samantha's cheeks.

Long into the night, talk between them went on, reminiscences and explanations. At last it was decided that all three of them would go to New York the next day, Mark having convinced Blaize and Samantha that he would be his own best representative to Anne-Marie Leighton. Thus it was that, late the next day, Samantha and Blaize stood anxiously in the hall outside Anne-Marie's bedroom, watching the tall, gaunt old man, a bouquet of roses in his hand, go through the door to meet the love he had not seen for almost thirty-six years. Samantha looked up and saw Blaize watching her, a terribly sad look in his beautiful dark eyes.

'What's wrong?' she asked softly. 'Are you afraid your mother won't want to talk to Mark?'

Blaize shook his head, and smiled. 'No. I was thinking how I'd feel if someone told me I wouldn't see you again until I was seventy years old.' He pulled Samantha into his arms and kissed her lovingly, then held her close. 'Shall we go to my study and sit down and wait?' he whispered into her ear.

'I'm too nervous to sit,' she whispered back.

'Let's pace up and down, then,' Blaize replied.

Hand in hand they walked up and down the thickly carpeted hallway, alternately interpreting the silence from Anne-Marie's room as ominous or comforting. Suddenly there was the sound of a woman's merry laughter, and Blaize stopped. He grinned down at Samantha.

'I haven't heard Mother laugh like that in years,' he said. 'Everything's going to be all right.'

Before Samantha could reply to his prophesy, the door opened and Mark Westland appeared.

'Come on in, you two,' he said, his smile as wide as Blaize's. 'I think it's time we got the whole family together.'

Samantha smiled up at Blaize, then, clutching his hand tightly, went to meet the woman who, many years before, had loved a man very much like Blaize with a passion that had threatened to tear her life asunder.

'Happy?' Blaize asked.

'Oh, yes!' Samantha said, leaning across him to wave out of the window as the limousine sped away from the lovely colonial church, its stark white steeple gleaming against the backdrop of fresh spring green trees. She wanted to imprint in her mind for ever the sight of the crowd gathered on the steps in the warm May sunshine. Mark and Anne-Marie Westland stood, arms around each other, blowing kisses to them. In deference to Anne-Marie's health, the two had married quietly as soon as Anne-Marie was able, but the warmth of Mark's love had done amazing things, and his wife was no longer the frail woman Samantha had first met. She was a tiny dynamo who had taken charge of making Blaize and Samantha's wedding as beautiful as any fairy-tale princess could have imagined. Bill Grimes had come, his generous heart so happy for Samantha that it overshadowed any bitterness he might have felt. Now, looking surprisingly dapper in his suit, he was smiling down at Monica Williams, who was clutching Samantha's bridal bouquet of pink and white roses, her eyes glued lovingly to Bill's face. Perhaps the roses were working their magic already! Samantha sighed and leaned back, her own eyes adoringly circling the handsome features of the man who was now her husband.

'Are you as happy as I am?' she asked.

'Twice as happy,' Blaize replied, chuckling as Samantha raised her eyebrows and pouted. 'Well, after all,' he went on, 'in the last two months I've gained not only the loveliest wife in the world but a real father, besides.'

Samantha nodded in understanding. 'I guess maybe that does double your happiness, doesn't it? It's extra happiness for me, too. I can still remember your face when you and Mark met for the first time. It was as if the sun had suddenly shone for you for the first time in a long, long time.' Her eyes misted as she recalled the meeting again.

'That's the way it felt,' Blaize said, his arms enfolding Samantha very tightly for a moment. Then he released her again and said thoughtfully, his eyes staring off into the distance, 'You know, it may sound a little odd, but I feel, in some strange way, as if Mark has always been a part of my life. There was a period, when I was a teenager, when I actually wondered if George Leighton was my father. We were so completely unlike each other. I used to imagine a father who laughed and told stories and loved life the way Mark does. I told Mark about that, and he told me that there was never a day of his life, after he got that note from my mother announcing I'd been born, that he didn't think of me and wonder what I was like, what I was doing. I don't think I really believe in ESP or psychic communication, but it does make you wonder, doesn't it?'

'It certainly does,' Samantha agreed. She leaned her head against Blaize's broad shoulder and put her forefinger on that telltale little cleft in his chin. That little clue had been there right from the beginning, but she hadn't known it meant so much. So many other things had had to fall into place. She sighed and smiled up at Blaize, who was watching her lovingly.

'A penny?' he said, taking Samantha's hands in his and idly caressing the finger where his ring now told of his troth.

'I was thinking of all the coincidences that had to happen to make this perfect day come about,' she said. 'If I hadn't agreed to do Mark's book, if you hadn't gone to California and turned on your television on that certain night, if the plumber hadn't left that open trench in my backyard ... there are so many. Do you suppose they really are just coincidences, or was it fate?'

Blaize chuckled and pulled Samantha into his arms.

'Let's call it fate,' he said. 'It's more romantic. Besides, who could ever prove us wrong?'

'No one. But it wasn't exactly fate that made George Leighton tell your mother that he'd told Mark about her and that Mark said he didn't give a darn.'

'No.' Blaize shook his head. 'I used to think that he loved her in his own strange way, and perhaps he did, but in reality it was more as if he wanted to possess her. It can't have been easy for him, knowing that she loved another man. I don't think I'll ever understand the motivation that made him so determined to protect the family name at the expense of both his and my mother's happiness. Mother apparently tried desperately to persuade him to call off their wedding. His ego just wouldn't permit it. My mother was supposedly the catch of the decade, what with her family's name and wealth, and her beauty besides.'

'Poor darling. She must have suffered so much.' Samantha raised her head, her eyes meeting those dark brown eyes she loved so very much, and smiling as that depth of communication that flowed so easily between them now made a warm glow fill her heart. 'You know, my love,' she said, letting the hands that always seemed to want to be touching this wonderful husband of hers have their way again to caress his cheek and then brush the thick, dark curls back from his forehead, 'if anyone were to tell me I had to marry someone else, I could never do it, no matter what the reason. I admire your mother's loyalty to her family, but I would walk across hot coals, climb the most terrifying peaks, or swim an entire ocean before I'd do it. They'd have to drag me to the altar, and even then I'd never say "I do".'

'It was a different world for women then,' Blaize said, sighing softly as Samantha tucked her hand between the buttons of his shirt and caressed him teasingly. 'Especially in an old, traditional family like hers, that placed such emphasis on doing things according to a certain form. Thank God she managed to keep me from being infected with their stuffiness.'

'I'm not sure she did,' Samantha replied, casting a sidelong glance at him. 'That was a pretty stuffy-looking gentleman who stood at my door with a box of roses one night not long ago.' She giggled as Blaize raised a questioning eyebrow at her.

'You thought I looked stuffy? I thought you were immediately convinced that I was a hopeless romantic.'

Samantha shook her head and began to unbutton his shirt. 'Not immediately. I thought you were a salesman, remember? And one that was trying to look very proper at that. I might never have found out differently if you hadn't fallen in that trench. I doubt if I'd have gone out with you if all you'd done was deluge me with roses and that romantic line of yours.'

'And I doubt if I'd have been so persistent if all I'd seen was that sophisticated-looking lady on the television. That adorable creature with the wispy hair, wrestling with her dog, was much more intriguing. And then there was the angel with the baseball bat in hand . . .' Blaize suddenly drew in his breath, and then retrieved Samantha's hand and carried her palm to his lips.

'Mmmm,' Samantha said dreamily, as the touch of Blaize's lips sent a shiver of desire through her. 'There's a lot more to our romance than roses, isn't there? But they'll always make me remember . . . so many things. Like the nights you called, and I pretended you were there with me. And the way Mrs McCarthy smiled when you handed her the bouquet. I think that's when I first began to understand that they could mean something very special, and that you were someone very special too.'

'That's what they're really for,' Blaize replied. 'They're just a symbol of all the things that two real people share. Their love, their dreams, sometimes their sorrow.' He gathered Samantha close and his lips found hers in a passionate kiss that lasted for a long time. When he raised his head, his eyes were glowing with a loving warmth, so strong that Samantha caught her breath, dazzled by the sight. 'We'll have many more roses, my darling,' he said softly. 'Our romance is only beginning.'

ATTRACTIVE, SPACE SAVING BOOK RACK

Display your most prized novels on this handsome and sturdy book rack. The hand-rubbed walnut finish will blend into your library decor with quiet elegance, providing a practical organizer for your favorite hard-or soft-covered books.

Only $9.95

**Approximately
16" x 8"
when assembled**

Assembles in seconds!

To order, rush your name, address and zip code, along with a check or money order for $10.70* ($9.95 plus 75¢ postage and handling) payable to *Harlequin Reader Service*:

Harlequin Reader Service
Book Rack Offer
901 Fuhrmann Blvd.
P.O. Box 1396
Buffalo, NY 14269-1396

Offer not available in Canada.

BKR-1A

*New York and Iowa residents add appropriate sales tax.

◆ Harlequin Romance

Coming Next Month

2953 BLIND TO LOVE Rebecca Winters
When Libby Anson joins her husband in Kenya, she's shocked by his announcement that their marriage is over. He insists that his blindness changes everything. But it doesn't—not for Libby.

2954 FETTERS OF GOLD Jane Donnelly
Nic is in love with Dinah. Although Dinah isn't as sure of her feelings for Nick, there's no way she'll let his overbearing cousin Marcus dictate what they can or cannot do!

2955 UNEXPECTED INHERITANCE Margaret Mayo
Alice is far from delighted at the prospect of a visit to the West Indies, all expenses paid. It means giving in to the commands of her unknown grandfather's will. Worse still, it means seeing Jared Duvall again....

2956 WHEN TWO PATHS MEET Betty Neels
Katherine is properly grateful to Dr. Jason Fitzroy for rescuing her from the drudgery of her brother's household and helping her to find a new life-style. She can't help dreaming about him, though she's sure he's just being kind.

2957 THE CINDERELLA TRAP Kate Walker
Dynamic Matt Highland doesn't connect the stunning model Clea with the plump unattractive teenager he'd snubbed years ago. But Clea hasn't forgotten—or forgiven—and she devises a plan to get even!

2958 DEVIL MOON Margaret Way
Career girl Sara is a survivor in the jungle of the television world, but survival in the real jungle is a different matter, as she finds out when her plane crashes. There, she is dependent on masterful Guy Trenton to lead the party to safety....

Available in January wherever paperback books are sold, or through Harlequin Reader Service:

In the U.S.
901 Fuhrmann Blvd.
P.O. Box 1397
Buffalo, N.Y. 14240-1397

In Canada
P.O. Box 603
Fort Erie, Ontario
L2A 5X3

Step into a world of pulsing adventure, gripping emotion and lush sensuality with these evocative love stories penned by today's best-selling authors in the highest romantic tradition. Pursuing their passionate dreams against a backdrop of the past's most colorful and dramatic moments, our vibrant heroines and dashing heroes will make history come alive for you.

Watch for two new Harlequin Historicals each month, available wherever Harlequin books are sold. History was never so much fun—you won't want to miss a single moment!

GHIST-1

◆ Harlequin Superromance

Here are the longer, more involving stories you have been waiting for... Superromance.

Modern, believable novels of love, full of the complex joys and heartaches of real people.

Intriguing conflicts based on today's constantly changing life-styles.

Four new titles every month.
Available wherever paperbacks are sold.

Harlequin American Romance

**Romances that go one step farther...
American Romance**

Realistic stories involving people you can relate to and
care about.

Compelling relationships between the mature men and
women of today's world.

Romances that capture the core of genuine emotions
between a man and a woman.

Join us each month for four new titles wherever paperback
books are sold.
Enter the world of American Romance.

Amro-1
